REVOLUTIONARY BABY

STRANGE TALES FROM THE TWENTIETH CENTURY

ANNETTE HAMILTON

This book is dedicated to my children Daniel Hamilton, Emma Hamilton and Obelia Modjeska, and to my granddaughters Lily Ann Anthony and Laluka Hamilton-Liebetreu.

And with special thanks and gratitude to my partner Michael Niblett.

NOTE TO THE READER

On spelling and grammar: most of the stories in this book are set in Australia and/or feature Australian characters. Australian writing and publishing conventions have been used. These are generally similar to those found in the United Kingdom but differ in some respects from United States' usage. There are some different spellings, grammatical forms and styles of punctuation. Use of word endings such as "..ise" instead of "...ize", spellings such as "labour" instead of "labor", and the placement of final full-stops outside rather than inside quotation marks are normal Australian usage.

CONTENTS

'THE FIRST REVOLUTION IS WHEN YOU CHANGE YOUR MIND'

Gil Scott-Heron, Interview in *High Times*, March
1977, 24.

1

———

BEYOND ENGAGEMENT

Sunlight pierced the blind and hit Judith's right eye. She shook herself and rolled over into the pillow. More sleep! The headache was still lodged behind her forehead. She needed water, she needed painkillers, she needed a different life. Then she remembered the essay. Was it finished? In her dreams she heard the typewriter keys, clack, clack, clack, over and over as the great stars wheeled overhead and the wind sighed through the gumtrees outside her window.

She opened both eyes. Yes, a neat pile of white pages sat on the old table, her desk. Her workspace. Where she worked on her not-work, her sham-work her mother called it, not real work, it didn't pay. The job in the milk bar paid all right but she couldn't stand it another moment. The Commonwealth scholarship to the university was a godsend but what would happen after she finished her degree?

She looked at the alarm clock, why hadn't she set it?

Maybe she did, maybe it didn't go off, maybe she didn't hear it. Ten thirty. Not so bad, she should still be able to get the twelve thirty train from Riverstone Station. She had been holding her breath without realising it. She did that a lot.

Somehow she went back to sleep, and there he was, her brother Bryan, trembling in his callipers.

'Wake up, wake up Judy, Mum needs you'.

Now she heard her mother's voice.

'Judy, Judy, get up, get out here, help me'.

A moment's silence.

'Judith, do you hear me? In the name of the Blessed Mother, get out here NOW'. Aileen's voice carried across two paddocks.

Bryan was pulling at her nightdress.

'Come on Judy, it's Grandpa, he's stuck on the dunny'.

She rolled over and pulled on her dressing gown, the pink chenille stained from the tea she couldn't help spilling while reading in bed.

'Okay, all right, I'm coming'. She hurried through the kitchen and out the back door, Bryan limping along behind her, snuffling through his nose, perpetually blocked, nobody knew why. Something to do with the polio, or hay fever, or asthma.

'Where's Dad and Callum?'

'Gone to the timber yard'.

Cormac O'Reilly ran a timber business, planing logs and selling off-cuts for firewood. His brother Callum helped him although he wasn't that much of a help on account of the metal plate in his head from the war against the Japs.

The pit-drop toilet was at the far edge of the garden. There was a proper plumbed one in the back of the house but the old man wouldn't use it. Or forgot where it was.

The door was open, she could see her mother pulling at his shoulders, trying to lift him.

'What happened?'

'Lord help us, can't you see? It's the usual thing with his back, he's slipped down and he's stuck. Here, you pull on this side'.

The familiar smell enfolded her. She didn't mind it that much, she'd grown up with it, the white lime her dad put down kept it sweet enough and mostly only grandpa went out there now except when there were visitors.

He struggled onto his feet, supported by Judith and Aileen.

'Come on Dad, you silly old thing'. He was Cormac's Dad, not Aileen's, but it was easier to call him that. Lately he didn't seem to recognise her anyway. He was in his tartan bedroom slippers, muttering.

'Mary, where's my Mary? Where are you my girl?'

Dead ten years, of the unspeakable C.

'Leave it, leave it, get off me, you ain't my Mary. Get off, I can manage now'.

But he couldn't. He was only sixty-six but weak and shrivelled, coughing from the thousands of roll-your-owns he had smoked since forever. Eamonn O'Reilly, stalwart of the early IRA until at 22 with the police after him he fled to Australia on a cargo boat, a fine specimen of a man but the booze got him and now his lights were almost out.

'There you go, me boys, fight for your freedom' he

shouted in the middle of the night. 'Down with the filthy British mongrel dogs!'

Mostly he was cheering on IRA actions, but sometimes he was marching among the ghosts of convicts from the Vinegar Hill uprising, led through the bushland by Aborigines to refuge in the valleys of the lower Blue Mountains. He talked about it as if it was right now, in 1962, even though it happened in 1804.

They knew he shouldn't be drinking but there was no stopping him. If home was dry, he'd disappear down the track to town and not come back, sometimes for days. Aileen or Cormac or Judith, or all of them, had to collect him in the horse-cart. Now at least they had a car, an old Holden, although only Cormac could drive it. He wouldn't let Aileen learn.

'No wife of mine will be seen driving a car!' he repeated too often down at the pub.

'Come on old fella, nearly there'. They supported him one on each side. Judith felt the pointy bones sticking out in his shoulders.

Eamonn stumbled along, wincing with pain.

'Me back, it's me back, girl, I need some of them powders' he muttered, and Judy could see red marks in the withered flesh where he'd been scratching at himself. What was wrong with him? Nobody knew for sure. They hardly ever went to doctors despite all their ailments. Aileen bought herbal remedies and oils from a local grocery shop, and there were plenty of painkillers on the shelves. Vincent's APCs were better than Bex but cost more.

They got the old man into the washroom. He'd gone in his pyjamas.

'Get a bucket of hot water'.

There was always hot water in the boiler over the fire. Mostly Aileen cooked on the fuel stove in the kitchen but kept the fire going outside, easy enough with the offcuts from the wood yard and a few logs dragged up from the creek. Judith came back with the bucket, shivering in her nightclothes.

'What are you up to, still abed at lunchtime? You should be ashamed of yourself'.

'I was up all night working on my essay'.

'Oh yes, working is it, of course you were'.

Judith winced. Her mother had no idea what she did night after night in her room, let alone what she did day after day at the university. She looked like her mother with her thick chestnut hair and pale skin and green eyes but sometimes her mother said she was a foundling from another realm.

'So beautiful but going on for twenty, and no sign of a blessed husband. No wonder when you hardly bother to wear a nice dress or put on makeup. Always with your nose stuck in a book'.

Judith started to go back to her room, but Aileen stopped her.

'Where do you think you're going now young miss?'

'I have to go into Uni today'.

'Today? It's Friday. Do you think I'm an idiot? You don't have classes on Fridays'.

'No but I have to hand my essay in'.

'Well and what is wrong with Monday? Surely it can make no difference to them. Your grandpa's messed his sheets. I need you to help me wash them, I've only got one spare set left'.

Washing sheets was almost the worst chore, apart from cleaning up after her brother and her grandpa. Her mother usually washed on Mondays, firing up the flames under the copper, turning the heavy linen around in the suds, rinsing it out, soaking it with the blue bag then wringing it through the mangle and hanging it on the line.

This year Judith was able to avoid it. She had English Honours on Mondays and caught the 7.30 am train. But with no more sheets, her mother would have to wash today.

She felt sorry for her mother, having to manage it all. Callum was supposed to help but he couldn't focus for very long and burnt himself in the boiling water more than once.

'Honestly, Mum, if I don't get the essay into the office by four I will fail. They stamp it with the date and time. My tutor told me, no further extension. They want to get rid of us, too many in the honours course.'

'So then what? Are you coming straight home?'

She was not. She had something even more compelling to do but she could not say a thing about it. It made her sick, the way she had to lie all the time.

'Yes, but I might be a bit late, I might run into some-one, or miss the train.'

Her mother shook her head. 'An empty sack does not stand' she muttered. She knew the girl was lying through her teeth, but was there any point in saying so? Maybe she had a boyfriend at the Uni. And that would be a good thing, would it not? Better for her to be married to someone with an education, someone with a better job, better prospects. If she stayed here in the Western

Suburbs working in the milk bar she'd probably finish up marrying some local jughead.

But on the other hand, a Uni man would be a man from somewhere else, a man who would take her daughter away. She loved her daughter with a fierce protectiveness. The thought of losing her was too awful. She prayed to the Blessed Mother every night that she could keep her beautiful girl nearby. A local jughead might be the better option.

'Well I expect you back by seven and no later. I'll keep your tea'.

'Yes, all right, okay ma, thanks, don't worry'.

She ran to her room and it was already noon. She would miss the express train. There was no time for a bath, just a quick wash under the arms and between the legs and plenty of talc and a spray of eau de cologne. She pulled on her tight black skirt and a pair of black stockings, tucked in her lemon shirt and pulled on a cardigan.

The essay! She wrapped it up in brown paper, she didn't have a plastic sleeve or a folder. She would buy one if the shop at Uni was still open. All the delicious-smelling heavy papers and pens and inks and new typewriters reminded her of what she so badly wanted but couldn't find the money for. She needed those things to become what she knew she really was, a writer, a writer of life, life as it is and not the fantasy life in silly books full of nonsense and dreams. She wanted to tell the truth about this life, what this time meant, these nineteen sixties, her time, she wanted to keep its stories real.

It was warm in the sun and she almost ran the mile to the station with her essay in a shopping bag banging against her thigh.

She barrelled up the stairs and saw the station was almost empty. Had she missed the later train as well? That would be a disaster. She wished she had a watch, that's why she was always late. A few people stood at the other end of the station, sheltering from the southerly wind whipping along the lines. She hurried forward and banged into a long-haired girl holding hands with a skinny pale fellow. They stopped, stared at each other.

'Sheila! Sheila Wells! It's you, isn't it?'

She looked at the swelling belly under the floral frock.

'Hullo Judy, yeah, it's me all right'. Her face lit up with a beatific smile and two missing teeth. 'How ya going?'

'Fine. Great. You?'

'Real good thanks. This is my fiancé Teddy' she said, pulling the man – boy really – forward and waving her hand in Judith's face, flashing what might or might not be a diamond ring.

'Hey, Teddy, this is Judy O'Reilly. We were mates in primary'.

'Yeah, good-O, how ya going?' Teddy said. But he clearly wasn't very interested.

'Hey, how about the train? Has it gone already?'

'No, no'. They looked to the west, where the train will come from. 'It's late'.

'Yeah, it's late'. Teddy dropped Sheila's hand and put his arm around her. Was he shy or cross?

'Thank goodness' said Judith, 'I thought I'd missed it. Going to the city?'

'No way, just to Blacktown, to see Teddy's dad. He got a new car. He's going to give us his old one'.

'You're a pair of lucky ducks'.

'Yeah, that's right, we are'. Sheila held her fine blonde hair down. She really was very pretty, beautiful even, apart from the teeth. Her skin flushed.

'So what are you doing?'

'Well, ah … not much. Had a job in a shop for a while'. She could not tell Sheila she was a Uni student. It wasn't shame, exactly, but there was something so unlikely about it. She didn't know what Sheila would think, let alone her blank-looking fiancé.

Should she ask when the baby was due, where they were living, when they were getting married? Maybe they hadn't even made those plans yet. A lot of people here did things without plans, they just let things happen. But pregnant, unmarried, in public? Even if some of the Catholic girls got pregnant while they were still at school they got married right away, you had to do that, the shame on the families was too much. Those babies were always born "early", you didn't have to count the months. Everybody knew it but nobody said anything. Otherwise, say for instance if the father of the kid shot through, the girl was sent away to a Catholic home and her baby was adopted. But then she remembered Sheila wasn't a Catholic anyway, that's why she'd gone to the local High school instead of St Benedicta's.

She was saved by the sound of the train rattling in. She definitely did not want to sit with them. It was obvious Teddy didn't want to sit with her either. He dragged Sheila off towards the back carriage.

'Bye' she called.

'Yeah, good luck, see you later'.

It was too weird, seeing her old school-friend with her

swollen belly and her engagement ring, looking so happy. It was the very worst thing Judith could imagine.

She sank into a seat and stared out the window. There were farms with horses and cows, gardens and fruit trees around the old weatherboard houses. It looked nice enough, beautiful even, but you couldn't tell from looking what went on in those houses, around those yards, in those gardens, behind those sheds. You had to live there to know.

Ever since her breasts appeared and she realised she was no longer a smart skinny girl with her head in the clouds but an actual grown-up woman she dreamed of the day when she wouldn't have to live out here. She wanted to live in the city, near the Uni, like all the other smart students in her course. She wanted to be free to get up whenever she liked, to go to the pub, invite people over for drinks and food, smoke cigarettes in bed.

When she started at Uni the year before she didn't know people actually did these things in Sydney. She knew they did them in London and Paris and other places she read about, but she found out there was already a life like that here, where people pleased themselves, worked or scrounged money, went around in groups, lived in share houses, young, strong, with definite opinions about everything, talked all the time, didn't care what anybody thought about them, sneered at the oldies, lived by a kind of code which wasn't exactly secret but had to be learnt. Some of them even had sex with each other and nobody cared if they were engaged or not. How did the girls not get pregnant?

The students in her English classes were more like

people in films and novels than the people she grew up with. When she got on the train she began the journey to being someone else. By the time she got off at Central, something had happened, the magic had worked. Her name now was Jude, not Judy or Judith, she was Jude the Obscure. It was a kind of a joke with herself, a deadly serious joke that she didn't dare tell anyone, until she told Tim one afternoon in the pub and then later Luca and neither of them laughed at her, instead she felt a kind of respect from them both.

Tim had given his first tutorial paper on Thomas Hardy's novel. She had never heard of it, they didn't teach Thomas Hardy at St Benedicta's even in the advanced class. She found a copy in the library and as she started reading she felt a jolt. It was about her, her existence, even though Jude Fawley was a young man and it all happened before the twentieth century even began. But there it was: Jude was a stonemason who wanted to become a scholar. She was a woodman's daughter and she not only wanted to become a scholar but she knew she would become a scholar, and more.

The plot of the novel was crazy and dense and complicated in that late Victorian way, but you could tell it was about people trying to pull away from what they were meant to do, from how they were meant to be, making their own rules and living by them, but it was hard and painful, and nothing went right for them. Now it was sixty years later, more than halfway through the century, and she would achieve what they could not.

And although she identified with Jude, she also thought about Sue, how she tried to avoid marriage and settling down and the rest of it, and as the grassy fields suddenly ended and turned into block after block of fibro and brick houses stretching north and south from the train line she realised that Sheila with her fiancé and pregnant belly was exactly the fate that she was determined to escape. Becoming Jude was an essential part of that.

She thought about how things had changed. For the first six months she struggled to understand what she had to do in the sandstone world. At first her clothes and her hair weren't right. Now every day on the train she loosened her ponytail and pulled it up into a French twist. Her mother had tried to make her wear step-ins and nylon stockings to Uni. But it was easy to convince her that there were too many stairs and cobblestones, and she laddered the stockings on the rough desks in the lecture theatres. It was all right for her to wear plain skirts and flat shoes. A few of the girls had turned up in pants this year, but she wasn't going to try that, at least not yet.

She had to change her voice. She sounded a bit Irish, but the Western Suburbs lay on top of it, the slowness, the mouth barely open, 'neooow' for 'now', 'stayers' for 'stairs'. The nuns had tried to stamp it out, St Benedicta's claimed its girls always spoke well, but here at Uni she was still too broad, too Australian. When she first tried to say something in tutorials she felt the other students as well as the staff dismissed her. She didn't want to sound too toffee either, that was just as bad, that private school thing. Now she had tamed her voice most of the time, although she had to watch it when she was drinking beer and arguing. Her long vowels slipped out all too quickly.

This train did not stop at Redfern, she would have to

catch a bus up Parramatta Rd to arrive in time. It was going slowly for some reason, there must be some holdup on the line. Her tutor made it perfectly clear that this was her last chance. He had been very generous even allowing her to rewrite the essay. He could have failed her, but he could see she hadn't understood what was expected. Giving her a new topic was doing her a favour, even though she'd have to do more reading. She thanked him profusely but the way he took her hand made her feel queasy.

The essay. She didn't want to think about it, wanted to think instead of what would happen afterwards, when she got to the meeting in the Philosophy Room and saw Luca's shiny black curls and blue-green eyes, when he smiled at her as she slipped through the crowd and slid into the seat he kept for her.

But now the essay was burning her mind. She needed to take another look at it, to read it over, even though she knew if she found anything wrong it was too late, impossible to fix up. Still, she couldn't help herself. She pulled open the string around the brown-paper package. And there was the title page neatly typed with the brand-new topic.

'*A good deal of Paradise Lost strikes one as being almost as mechanical as bricklaying*'. F. R. Leavis, 1936. Evaluate the relevance of this observation to Pope's *Essay on Criticism* paying particular attention to prosody and metaphor'.

She hadn't understood what had been wrong with her first essay. '*Select a poet who addresses issues of criticism and criticise their work or works*'.

She had chosen Pope's poem, which she liked a lot, and focused her discussion on one stanza.

The Vulgar *thus through imitation err;*
As oft the Learn'd by being singular;
So much they scorn the Crowd, that if the
  Throng
By Chance *go right, they* purposely *go wrong:*
So Schismatics the plain Believers quit
And are but damn'd for having too much wit.

This meant that poets usually want to impress by either copying something or doing the opposite so as to make themselves seem more important. Critics needed to know the difference. She argued that to do this, the critic had to understand the biography of the poet, the history and social context of the poem. This seemed so self-evident that she couldn't understand the tutor's comments. She was relieved that he had allowed her to write the new essay using Pope, but she still had no idea what she had done wrong.

She had never heard of F. R. Leavis. She read some of his articles and when she finally grasped what he was on about she thought it was idiotic. Leavis said that there was no role in criticism for philosophy, biography or history. The only thing that mattered was the text itself, the words on the page. In one of his famous comments he said that the critic must 'attain a peculiar completeness of response in order to enter into possession of the given poem in its concrete fullness'. Whatever that meant.

Someone had to sift out the dross of bad writing and establish the elements of the good, which was supposed to revitalise a nation's cultural health. It seemed a tall order. She liked poetry, loved it even, but she hardly thought a few poems were going to remedy the deficiencies in the everyday world or fix up society.

Pope could be dismissed because of his long stanzas, regular rhythms and rhyme schemes, laid like bricks, so his work, just like Milton's, could not belong to the canon of poetic greatness.

She couldn't take it seriously. Of course there was good and bad poetry, good and bad writing, but it was up to the readers to decide that, not a refined and elevated person from some snobby British university.

She had toiled and struggled and done tricky things with her sentences and doubled back on her own position, so it was clear she understood what the question intended without agreeing with it. Writing that essay had made her feel slippery and unclean. Why should she have to turn herself inside out because some fuzzy little tutor with a grating accent had power over her entire future? All he wanted her to do was parrot some blatherer who claimed superior authority over the views of mere colonials.

Rereading the essay in the train made her angry and upset all over again. She could see it was not a good essay, how could it be when she didn't agree with what they were making her write? And even if she did pass, did she really want to spend more time and energy doing the same kind of thing just to stay in the course? What was the point, when she wanted to be a writer herself, not some parasitic critic? And now the train was pulling into Central, and she had to put the essay back into the package and tie it up with string and she realised that only an absolute hick would hand it in like this.

SHE RAN AS FAST as she could, but her skirt was too tight. It was only a couple of minutes before the deadline. She rushed across the pathway off the main quadrangle and up the creaking dark wooden staircase to the English office. 'Miss Nora Fanshell, Secretary' was written in elaborate gold script.

The door was shut. She knocked. No answer. She walked up and down the corridor, hoping to hear a voice or catch a glimpse of someone. Dust motes shimmered against the stained-glass window, beautiful. She went back to the door and knocked again, put a hand on the brass knob, the door opened. Amazing. The secretary hadn't gone home yet.

The click-clack of high heels came up the stairs and a rush of gratitude made her want to hug the woman wearing them. Which would be unthinkable. Still, she babbled her relief. Miss Fanshell stared as she handed over the brown paper parcel.

'I don't know if I can accept this' she said, turning it over in her hand as if it might be dangerous. 'Dr Selby almost certainly won't'. She squinted up at Jude. 'You are sure he gave you an extension to today?'

'Yes, he did. I know it should be in a sleeve, but the train was late, and I didn't have time to buy one and anyway the shop was shut'.

'It is Friday afternoon and people do want to get home'.

'Yes, I understand. I'd be so grateful if you could accept it. Maybe I could come in on Monday morning with a proper sleeve. I promise I will! If you could just stamp it? On the cover sheet?'

Miss Fanshell looked at the empty emerald lawn. Then she turned back with a kindly expression, not quite a smile.

'These things happen. I have a spare folder here somewhere. I'll just clip it in, that will be fine I'm sure'.

She unwrapped the essay, stamping the front sheet with the date and time. Jude realized Miss Fanshell was sorry for her. Just as well. It was a close thing.

'Thank you so much, you are so kind, I can't tell you how much I appreciate it'.

'That's all right. Some of our students have a much harder time of it than others. Please close the door on your way out'.

Jude was so relieved that the pity behind the statement didn't quite register. She ran down the stairs and hurried along the cloisters to the Philosophy Room where the meeting would have been going for an hour at least. She smelled it first, the dense fog of tobacco smoke drifting up the staircase. Then she heard the voices clamouring, an argument of some kind. There must have been fifty people in the room, mostly men she had never seen before. Student Action had been a small group, up to now at least.

She looked for Luca. She knew he would be angry with her for being so late. He said more than once that he expected her to be there so she could say something and then vote with him. It was a crucial vote. She was meant to represent the girl student perspective. He didn't say it quite like that but the intention was obvious.

She caught sight of Luca down the front of the room, with Dave Delgado. Dave was shouting at the speaker, his fist clenched. Max Armytage was shouting back and there was a banner strung up behind him with red writing: *Students for Revolutionary Action*. The movement had been renamed. Jude did not dare go down the front to join them. Tim, the red-headed boy from her English class, was sitting in the far corner at the back. There was a free seat next to him, so she went over and took it. She felt strangely connected to him. He was from the Western Suburbs too. His dad was a famous union leader. They used to live in Balmain until the Housing Commission sold their houses and made them move to the distant west.

'Good grief! What are you doing here?'

'Why wouldn't I be here?'

'I didn't think you were political'.

'Well I'm not really. Or maybe I am. I don't know'.

She knew Tim liked her. He offered her a Peter Stuyvesant. It was considered quite a glamorous cigarette.

'Glad you are here anyway' he said, 'What a circus!'

'Why, what's happened?'

The whole room was buzzing with stir and uncertainty. A few older men were standing around the back of the room. Tim pointed them out.

'See them? They're ASIO, Security and Intelligence spooks pretending to be students. Not bloody likely with those haircuts'.

The shouting grew louder. Max brandished a thick wad of papers, getting ready to read.

The room was divided, some cheering Max on, others booing.

'But what happened?' she asked.

'It's the new Engagement Committee. Supposed to work out what the Students for Revolutionary Action are going to do. Max has been voted in as leader. Luca – wait, you know Luca don't you, you've been going round with him?'

'Well, kind of'.

'Anyway, Luca was voted in as Deputy, but it was supposed to be Dave. He's so pissed off that he just resigned from the Committee altogether, Dave that is. Max ruled him ineligible because he isn't a student'.

'But that's not fair! He's only been suspended'.

Dave was a brilliant philosophy student and Luca's best mate. As editor of the student newspaper he had supported a student action defacing the big war memorial in the city. The Disciplinary Committee had taken such a dim view of it that he had been suspended for a term, 'stood down' they called it.

Now Max was speaking, and the room went quiet.

'As the first business of the Engagement Committee I propose that we carry forward the action that our comrade Dave Delgado began last year. We will focus on Anzac Day which as we all know will be on Thursday next week'.

Anzac Day, when the entire nation stops to remember the war-dead, was the most sacred day in Australia's calendar.

'We must protest against the glorification of war and militarism and Australia's craven submission to the United States of America! We must mobilise against the domination of capitalist imperialism wherever it appears! We must reject nuclear war! Our government is under the thumb of the USA! We used to kow-tow to Britain's every whim, now it's the USA pulling our chain. In war after war we have been the disposable troops, the colonial sacrifices. This must stop!'

The room erupted into cheering.

'We must undertake firm revolutionary action' he said. 'Solidarity forever!'

'Solidarity forever! Solidarity forever! Down with Uncle Sam!' Cheers and shouts filled the room, people were on their feet, an electricity was in the air. One or two of the men at the back were trying to disguise the fact they were taking photographs, their cameras hidden underneath their coats.

The cheering went on. Dave Delgado stood. His dark eyes flashing, his hair tied at the back of his neck, he was almost shaking.

'So what do you propose we do? What will be our initial revolutionary action?' A look of pure hatred passed across his face. Jude had never seen this version of him before.

'Ahh, comrade, that is a matter for the Committee' Max said, 'not something we can discuss here.'

'But how will everyone get our instructions? So they know where to go, what to do?' A tiny wiry girl was standing on her chair. Rachel Liebling, everybody knew her with her bushy red hair tied on top of her head, she was the most brilliant of the Third Year Philosophy students. 'We can't just stick notices up on the noticeboard'.

'We are developing our communication strategies, dear comrade Rachel, new and effective methods. Everyone will hear in good time'. He jutted his chin toward the ASIO spies at the back wall. 'In confidence'.

Jude realised that Max was somehow attractive. His voice was compelling. He talked up a storm.

'The Committee will convene later' he said. 'But first, let's all have a drink together. We will see a new dawn, and it starts at the march next week! Solidarity forever!'

They usually met at the downstairs bar of the Australia Hotel in Chippendale. On a nice day they could sit out in the beer garden. When it was cold and windy the bar inside was cosy with an open fire and plenty of privacy. It was small enough to see everyone who came in. And, very unusually, the hotelier let women drink at the same bar as the men. The students more or less took it over after one of their meetings.

But it was still a public bar. And if ASIO was openly attending their meetings at the University they would surely know where they went to drink. And what if one of the students on the Committee was actually a spy? It was perfectly possible.

The action at the Cenotaph in March 1960 had brought fury down on the students. Not that Jude was around at the time, it was two years before she even started at Uni, but it was one of those events that everyone remembered and talked about, and Dave and Luca had both been involved from the start. It happened at the usual wreath-laying ceremony to mark Coral Sea Week and celebrate US-Australian relations.

The Tribune said that US military personnel were flying secret combat missions into North Vietnam and bombing innocent villagers. The Americans called the Viet Cong "insurgents" but the comrades in the Student Movement said they were just patriots trying to defend their own country. The Tribune was a communist news-paper. Was it right to believe what it said?

All she had heard her whole life that the Americans had been the saviours of Australia.

"Saviours, I tell you, saviours! If they hadn't turned up at the Coral Sea, we'd all have been Japanese prisoners-of-war". Her uncle would down another rum and tears would run down his cheeks. It happened every Anzac Day.

She'd grown up hearing the same thing from everyone. It wasn't so long ago. The war in the Pacific was so painful, prolonged, violent, cruel. Lots of men around the district were lost on the Burma-Thailand railroad, others were returned soldiers who spent Anzac Day getting drunk on their memories. The Japs almost made it but then the Americans arrived and fought them to a stand-still. In the end it was the atom bomb that finished it off. Everyone said although it was horrible it was no more than the Japanese deserved.

Until she went to university, she never questioned this story. Her dad and her uncle should know, they were there, and although they fought with each other it was because they disagreed about the US general, Douglas MacArthur: her dad thought he was a slimy coward, her uncle thought he did better than anyone else could have done.

Some articles she read in the Tribune said that the Japanese never meant to invade Australia in the first place and condemned the Americans for using the bomb at all. Now a lot of students were anti-nuclear as well as anti-war and the Campaign for Nuclear Disarmament was getting stronger all the time. There were more and more protests at US foreign policy and the way it was going, especially in Southeast Asia. President Kennedy had intervened in South Vietnam to stop the Communists from taking over. And the world was on the brink of nuclear war at the Bay of Pigs. It was all too terrifying. People thought for sure it was the end of the world. That movie *On the Beach* had scared her, and everyone else, witless.

There were good reasons to demonstrate. But she couldn't help thinking the Uni students went in for silly stunts. In 1960 they released a red-painted greased pig in the crowd. A few old servicemen were knocked over. Thirteen students were detained, the University authorities were pressed to act against the students but there seemed no reasonable grounds for doing so.

It was easy for them to blame Dave Delgado after he wrote editorials supporting the student action. He was told to publish an apology and refused. He went on publishing anti-US articles and this made him an easy target. But it was only a short suspension, it could have been a lot worse. Michael Kirby, president of the Student's Representative Council, came out in support of the students. The Tribune quoted him: he praised the 'awakening of student concern with recurrent social and political problems facing them as intelligent members of the community'. That was quite a boost for Dave and Max and the others.

Jude suddenly realised the meeting was breaking up. It was so smoky that she could hardly breathe. They were still chanting: 'Down with US Imperialism', 'Support Revolutionary Action', 'Solidarity Forever' as the meeting broke up and Jude saw a chance to get to Luca who was hurrying to catch up to Dave, already out the door.

'Luca, Luca' she called but he didn't stop and seemed not to have heard her. She headed him off and put her hand on his arm. He stopped suddenly while others streamed around them.

'Where were you?' he said. 'I told you to be here. We needed your vote'.

'It wouldn't have made much difference, would it?'

'It might have. Anyway, I need to be able to rely on you'.

'All right, I'm sorry, the train was late and then there was nobody at the office'.

'At the office? What office?'

'I told you, I had to hand in my English essay'.

'So that's more important than this?'

He was walking on. She followed, feeling ridiculous. She thought he would be angry but not like this.

'I'm sorry, I'm sorry. Can we have dinner tonight? I want to talk to you'.

'Are you dim or something? Didn't you just hear that the Committee will be meeting tonight?'

'Well can't I come along?'

He glared at her. Was it contempt on his golden face?

He pushed forward through the crowd.

'Scuse me, scuse me, make way there, thanks. Hang on a bit. Dave, Dave' he called, and they came up the stairs and saw Dave sitting on the sandstone balustrade. He was pale and tense. They were pushed by the mass of students spilling up the worn stone steps. Dave looked at Jude.

'Why weren't you here? Luca said we could rely on you'.

She started to explain but Luca cut her off.

'Come on, let's go to the pub, we can talk there'.

They crossed the lawn and walked down toward Victoria Park in the cool evening breeze. Jude was seething with anger. How dare they treat her like this, as if she didn't matter? But then, maybe she didn't matter. Luca and Dave were deep in conversation. She hesitated, stopped in the middle of the pathway, wondering if she should give this whole evening up and go home. It would make her mother happy.

She was still trying to make up her mind when Max came up behind her. He touched her shoulder gently and when she turned, surprised, she saw a sparkle in his eyes and a warm smile. She was so relieved to see a friendly face that she smiled back, and then they were going along to the pub together and Luca didn't even notice, striding along beside Dave, their heads together.

She felt a rush of emotion, of longing and disappointment and confusion. She had been so happy getting close to Luca. For months they had been meeting once or twice a week for lunch or coffee. She helped him out by typing his position papers for the Committee. In fact she was editing and rephrasing a lot from his cramped handwriting. He wrote well but made a lot of grammatical mistakes. At first he said not to change anything, but she made the sentences flow and soon he barely looked at the final version, that was how much he trusted her. She was in the cramped office most days, typing, filing things, making the tea.

Luca was famous on-campus. Going round with him gave her status with the other students. People said she was his girlfriend. She wanted to be more than his girlfriend. She wanted to be his fiancée. It would resolve so much. Her parents might even let her move into town if they knew she was engaged. He would have to meet them of course. But she thought that would go all right.

Luca came from an Italian family so they were Catholics too, not that Luca ever went to church or anything, but it would make it easier for her mother to accept him. He could be kind and polite when he wanted to, and he was so good-looking, with his long eyelashes and smooth golden skin.

Then something like this happened and she feared he didn't care for her in that way at all. He would hold her hand and put his arm around her, but was that enough? Sometimes he would lean in, as if seeing her for the first time, and it felt like electricity between them. But then he would pull away and she wondered if she was dreaming. Was this falling in love? She longed for him to kiss her properly, not just a gentle press on the lips but a full-blown kiss with the tongue and the rest of it, like in the movies. What did he feel? How could she tell? Should she go on hoping? Or, if he was not that interested, cut her losses? She thought she loved him, but maybe not that much.

She saw the pair of them, Luca and Dave, sloping along down the hill in their relentless conversation. She couldn't help thinking Luca liked Dave a lot more than he liked her.

Max was talking, but she wasn't really focusing on what he was saying because she was watching Luca. Then she realised he was talking about his former girl-friend, Seraphim Steele. Everybody knew her. She was outrageous, with her wild curly hair and vivid speech littered with profanities like a wharfie. She was a total star in the English Department, even some of the lecturers fawned over her. She had come up from Melbourne with Max but didn't hesitate to leave him when offered a student place at a top English University. One day she was performing some wild drama, the next she was gone.

'I do miss her so much' Max said. 'She was such an exciting person to be with. Every day with her was an adventure. But then again, it was tiring. And I never knew what was going on between us. She spreads herself very thin'.

'Really? What do you mean exactly?'

There was hurt in his eyes. They arrived at the pub, Luca and Dave were already sitting in the far corner with three men, strangers to her.

Max led her to a table near the entrance. 'Why don't we sit here for a bit?' he smiled. 'I'd like to get to know you better'.

She sat obediently but was watching the others, trying not to be obvious about it. Dave had his notebook open and was writing in it, someone else arrived with a jug of beer and some glasses. Dave and Luca smiled at each other, clinked their heavy glasses, sloshing with froth.

Jude didn't get it. Luca and Dave seemed to be closer than ever, even though Luca has agreed to be Max's deputy and Dave loathed Max, mainly because he was a Melbourne Trot. That was a main issue, apparently. What made a Melbourne Trot different to some other one?

Jude tried to understand. She knew that a Trot was a follower of Leon Trotsky, a Marxist theorist and revolutionary. Trotsky was assassinated in Mexico in 1940 after a passionate affair with that weird-looking woman artist with the single eyebrow.

'Beer?' Max hovered over her. 'Something else? You're Irish, do you prefer whisky?'

'Beer thanks. How do you know I'm Irish?'

He laughed. 'Not hard to work that out. Won't be a moment'.

He disappeared inside while Jude waited. A couple of others from the meeting asked if they could sit down.

'Of course' she said. 'But I'm waiting for Max'.

'Oh' they said. 'Well, better move on then. See you later'.

She caught the brief hesitation, the doubt in their eyes. What was she doing sitting with Max? She was supposed to be Luca's girlfriend. Would this cause trouble? For a moment she thought of going to Luca's table and pulling up a chair and sitting down next to him. She could do that. He would have to talk to her then. But it mightn't go well. Luca could be mean. She knew to be careful around him, watch what she said, anticipate his reactions. Right now, he obviously did not want to be with her. She knew he would be cross when she didn't get to the meeting on time, but this cold shoulder was far worse than she expected.

Now here she was, sitting with Max. She wasn't even sure Luca had seen them, but she knew Dave had. His scowl in her direction was brief but focused. But there was something in her now. She was tired of trying to make everyone else happy. She was tired of having to lie all the time. She wanted to just be herself, do what she felt like. There was not one person on the face of the earth except maybe poor little Bryan who accepted her just as she was.

Everyone wanted her to be something else, something

more, something less: quieter, more helpful, more atten-tive. She was sick of working out what they all wanted and how to give it to them, she was sick of putting on an act. When she read great poetry, or wonderful books, she felt she was right there with the author, as if they instantly understood each other, and the rawness of the writer's experience was shared so she could respond. But here in her real life, nobody seemed interested in giving her anything, sharing anything. They wanted her to under-stand how to make them happy and then do it without a murmur.

Max came back with a jug of beer and two glasses. He sat and poured, the froth thick and lustrous on top. She liked beer, but not that much. And it was getting cold. The late afternoon southerly stirred the leaves around the garden.

'I'm cold' she said. 'Can we go inside?'

Max immediately stood up and she started to pick up her bag, but he slipped his pea-jacket off and walked around the table, putting it carefully over her shoulders.

'There' he said, 'Is that better? I don't want to go inside just yet, everyone is talking, it's so noisy and smoky'.

'Okay, yes, thanks'. She lit a cigarette, offered him one. He shook his head.

'You don't smoke?'

'No, but I don't mind or anything, feel free'.

'How come?'

'Oh well, you know … my family was pretty much against it. I tried a few times but it made me cough. I had a bit of lung trouble'.

She wants to ask more, but he pulled away, like most men he would not talk about his weaknesses.

'So who did you vote for today?'

'What do you mean?'

'For the Engagement Committee. It is a bit of a shame, really, but it wouldn't be right for Dave to be on it. I mean, he isn't really a student, is he?'

'Well I don't know. Does it matter what it says on some form or other? He's been a student for years'.

'Yes, that's true. But that's a problem too. I mean a student is meant to graduate. Even when they do go part-time. You can't be a student for ever'.

'Anyway, I didn't vote. I got there too late'.

'Really? What happened'.

Max seemed genuinely interested. He poured her more beer, and suddenly Jude found herself telling him about the essay, the tutor, her confusion, her problem of not knowing what to do to pass the course.

He listened. Over in the corner she saw Luca and Dave stand, pick up their jackets, head into the lounge bar. Luca hadn't paid the slightest attention to her.

'So I finally rewrote it, I had to stay up all night, then my Mum needed help with my grandpa. I got a later train and then that was held up and I only just got there and the Secretary wasn't in the office. Now I don't even know if I'll pass or not. I just don't get what they are on about.'

Max took her hand gently.

'Don't worry about those clowns. The new professor just got here last year, it's one of the reasons Seraphim was so keen to piss off. You'll see, they won't last, but in the meantime, you're caught in the middle. I'd get out of it as soon as I can if I were you. Pick another subject, you're only in second year, it won't matter. You could do philosophy, or politics'.

'Yes, but I want to be a writer'.

'Well, doing English isn't going to help with that. What you need is life experience. And being part of the revolution will definitely count!'

She wasn't sure if he was teasing her. But he seemed serious enough.

'And make sure you get to the Anzac Day action next week. Someone will tell you about it. Luca probably'.

'I don't know. He mightn't. I don't have a phone and I won't be in at Uni this week, I have to help out at home'.

'Oh. Well, it's not confirmed and we're keeping it quiet but I'm sure you're not ASIO'. He laughed. 'We're meeting near the front of the march before it starts. With banners and so on. As soon as it sets off we'll slip in front of them and go along as far as we can before they stop us'.

She stared at him.

'Really? They won't let us do that. We'll be arrested'.

'Maybe. But we will have made our point. Someone has to'.

Jude shivered. She did not want to do this. People were getting more and more upset about Anzac Day. She thought about last year, the drama at home. Her Dad wanted to go to the march, her uncle didn't, they start to argue and soon they were shouting at each other, and then they went off to the pub to play two-up but they kept on drinking and got arrested for drunk and disorderly.

She tried to explain all this to Max. He was listening, his eyes on her face, stroking her hand gently while he drank his beer. The jug was almost empty.

'I don't want to stay here' Jude said suddenly. 'It's too cold. I think I should go home'.

'But it's still early. How about some dinner? Would you like that?'

She realised suddenly she would. She had not eaten all day.

'Well yes, okay, maybe that's a good idea'.

The two of them were almost alone in the beer garden now, the lights were off, everyone else was inside.

'Well good, let's do it. Let's go to the Greeks, is that okay?'

'Yes', she said, and it was. She thought of the scent of garlic and rosemary and oil and the soft lamb falling off the bones. 'That's a great idea'.

'But I need to go home first, to drop off my things. It's right near here'.

Her head was spinning as she stood up. Max put his hand out to steady her, and smiled, a strange, triumphant little smile. But she didn't want to think about it, just wanted to do something decisive, make a choice no matter how it turned out.

They left the pub and walked along Abercombie Street for a couple of blocks. The windows looked blankly out at the busy street, a few broken toys on a doorstep, straggly shrubs in gardens which hadn't been looked after in years. Then they turned into a side street and Max had a key in his hand and opened the door of a three-story terrace house on the high side of the street. The peeling paint and rotting windowsills could not disguise the elegance of the old building, a wrought iron balcony above.

She followed Max inside. She badly needed to pee. The toilet was out the back.

'Come upstairs when you're ready'.

She went through a gloomy kitchen with a sink full of

dirty dishes. There was an odour of – what – garbage? A stopped-up drain? But outside there was a little garden with some herbs and veggies, and a couple of iron chairs. Nice in good weather. She thought: I could live in a place like this if I left home.

She peed at last, such a relief. There was no toilet paper. Fortunately she had some rolled up in her handbag. The sink consisted of a garden hose propped up on a metal grid outside the door.

Inside the house it was almost dark. A main stairway led in one direction, a narrower one in another, there was music playing somewhere.

'Where are you?' she called.

'Here' Max replied. 'Upstairs'.

She went up the main staircase.

'Where?'

'Here'.

A door was open a chink. She pushed it in. Max stood looking out the grimy window. He wore only a pair of grey pants. The room was chaotic, clothes strewn all over the floor, more in a bulging wardrobe. Cardboard boxes and wooden crates full of papers and books were stacked up in every corner. It stank, in that strange single-man way of rooms almost never cleaned or tidied.

'So come on in' he said, turning around, smiling. Now he looked like a wolf.

There was nowhere to sit, except the bed. Her head was spinning again, she needed to lie down.

'Is someone else here?' She heard music from somewhere on the upper floor.

'Don't know. Yes, probably. Maybe Gabor, he's been staying with Effie.'

She didn't know these people. Max walked towards her with a bottle and a tumbler.

'Here, have some of this. It's a Hunter Valley'.

The idea of drinking red wine from a filthy glass turned her stomach.

'No thanks' she said. 'Let's get going'.

Actually she wasn't hungry anymore. All she wanted was to get out of there. This version of Max was scary, especially the smile.

'Oh, come on, plenty of time'.

He poured the wine and held it out. 'Just a little drinkie'.

She took the glass and cleared a space on the night table among the papers and notes and bits of cardboard. She was turning back when she realised he was standing right behind her.

'Come on then darling' he said, 'How about a bit of a cuddle'. And pushed her down onto the tangled grey sheets, holding her there with a sinewy hand.

'Let me go, get off me'.

But he was pushing himself down, trying to drag her skirt up to her waist and pawing at her panties. She could hear him breathing, almost wheezing.

'You know you like it, give us a go'.

She pushed him off her, screaming. He was surprised, and fell on the floor but righted himself and leapt up. Jude grabbed her bag, got to the door and pulled it open.

'Get the hell away from me' she yelled but he was coming after her and she stumbled and slipped on the top stairs. She could hear him behind her, his mad panting, 'Come on darling, come on darling'. And she could feel him reaching out for her, so she took the last few stairs in one leap, and felt her ankle twist underneath her as she fell.

Then there was another person holding her hand, pulling her up.

'Leave her alone you lowlife'. It was an older man with long curly brown hair and strong arms and shoulders. He pulled her away from the staircase and stood between them.

'Can't you see she's just a girl. And she doesn't want it. You hear me? She doesn't want it! If she says no, she says no'.

There was a deep anger in his voice, a European accent.

'What's it got to do with you?' demanded Max.

'Everything' he said and lifted his arm at the end of which was a fist and with the fist he hit Max's face and Jude thought she could hear bone breaking.

Max slumped to the floor, yelling. 'You broke my nose! You scum, you broke it'.

The man took her arm and led her to the front door.

'He is a very angry man, that Max, and not good to women'.

'Who are you?' asked Jude.

'I am Gabor' he said'.

'Thank you, thank you.' Strangely she wasn't crying. All she could think of was how to get away from this horrible place.

'I need to get home'.

'Yes, you do. Do you go by bus, train?'

'By train'.

'Good, I will take you to Redfern Station'.

'Thank you'.

'Here, take my jacket. It is cold'.

It was a beautiful brown leather jacket, soft, like a glove.

'Only till we get to the station' she said.

'No, you can take it home with you, you have had a shock, you mustn't get chilled. You can return it to me later'.

'But how will I find you? I don't want to come back here'.

'No, you don't. Just go to the Refectory and ask for Gabor. Everybody knows me.'

'Are you a student?'

'No, but I was a teacher once. I like to be at the University. I am hoping they will let me do another degree one day. Meanwhile I work on the docks. And play cards'.

Jude wanted to thank him a hundred times over as they hurried along in the cold wind.

'Why are you helping me? Are you a Christian?'

Gabor laughs.

'No, not a Christian. Just a man who loves freedom, believes people have the right to do what they want as long as it doesn't hurt others. And a duty to protect people so they don't lose their liberty'.

There was so much to ask but they were almost at the station entrance. An Aboriginal woman carrying a sleeping baby held out her hand. Many Aboriginal people lived here. Once Redfern was a market garden where fresh produce was sold to the locals who worked in the markets, the railways, in meat works and factories; now the place was derelict and there was no work. But the people were still here, surviving.

Gabor pulled some cash out of his pocket. He handed it to the woman, who grinned with white teeth.

'Good on you brother' she said.

'You're welcome" he replied.

There was a train approaching, going west.

Jude started towards the steps.

'I've got to go. Thanks so much Gabor. I promise I'll find you as soon as I can. Your jacket …'

'That's all right' he said. 'Anyway I can always get another jacket'.

She just made it onto the train. Luckily she had a return ticket. Gabor was standing next to the Aboriginal woman, chatting.

Jude sat in a window seat and watched the city unfurl behind her. She had been rescued, not just from the hideous Max, but from her own stupid self who had let this situation happen, who drank too much and never really understood what she was meant to do in this new world where she didn't belong. But that's how it was. There were others who didn't belong either, maybe they could make it so they belonged to each other.

She wanted a revolution all right but it wasn't one with slogans and arguments and men fighting each other over who was top dog in the pack. She wanted a revolution where people looked out for each other, the way Gabor looked out for her, where people were free and defend each other's freedom, took care of the weak, gave each other what they needed. She hated to think what was happening in Southeast Asia and it made sense that the Vietnamese wanted a revolution for themselves, but could that only mean violence? How could there be a revolution when there were madmen with atom bombs around every corner?

She didn't know about Anzac Day, but she believed her father when he said he fought for freedom, so she definitely wasn't going to demonstrate against that. The leather jacket was too big for her but she pulled it around her body and decided that when her mother asked her where she got it she will simply tell her the whole truth. And that would be the biggest freedom of all.

2

———

REVOLUTIONARY BABY

It was one of those mornings. Sweat dripped down Cliff's neck. He hated the feeling, so low and animal. His hair was too long, his last gesture of defiance against the Man. Stupid really. Zinc powder was meant to stop the itchy pustules under his starched white shirt, but it just made his skin white. In the misted mirror he looked like a corpse.

Now he ate cornflakes with sliced banana, cold milk and a sprinkle of sugar. Andrea was messing around in the bathroom. Water rushed on then off again. He couldn't understand how anyone could take so long washing. Apparently it was the pregnancy. All of her seemed to be exuding something: there was a constant scent, not unpleasant exactly but still raw, earthy.

He tried to be affectionate but in truth he felt repulsed. At night she lay snoring by his side, heaving under the sheet. He couldn't help thinking of corpses again. How was it that he, Cliff Meadows, lead singer of early punk band the Hijackers and undeniably a star of sorts had turned into a suburban solicitor with a pregnant wife in a cramped apartment? It happened so fast.

He finished his breakfast and started cleaning the plates. The sloshing slimy water reminded him of birth. Andrea said he had to be there. Her doctor said this was not advisable, but Andrea insisted. The father needed to identify through the birthing process and bond with the baby. No man he knew had ever been at a birth, except for one of his cousins who was an ambulance officer. Surely it was women's business. When Andrea pressed him as to why he was so reluctant he said didn't want to get in the way.

He couldn't tell her the two things that terrified him. The first was that the sight of her intimate parts all stretched out of shape and covered in blood and fluids would put him off sex forever. The second was simpler. He was certain he would faint, or shit his pants, or both.

The clock was ticking but still Andrea did not appear. Normally she made his lunch. He liked brown bread with salad and cheese or ham. He wanted her to make his lunch no matter what. In some way it was a small recompense for what his life had become. Plus it was cheap.

He earned enough but he didn't want to waste it. Dick, his best mate at work, had convinced him to buy stocks with any spare cash he had. Reluctantly at first, and then with increasing enthusiasm, he began following the market and reading the financial pages. Andrea didn't know and he would make sure she never found out. She would be so disapproving. It was bad enough that he was a solicitor, which meant working for the Man. How much worse if she found out he was investing in the System.

Finally, Andrea rushed in through the door. She was sporting overalls with a bib front like a boilermaker. Her belly stuck out, she looked like she'd had a lifetime drinking beer.

'What on earth are you wearing?' He knew at once it was the wrong thing to say.

'Clothes' she said. She went over to the counter and pulled out the bread, went to the fridge and found the cheese and salad things, already peeled and sitting in a crisper where Cliff had put them the night before to make it easier for her. He watched her broad hips under the heavy denim.

'But why …?' Should he go on with this conversation or just take his lunch and get out of the kitchen? He knew the answer, but it was too late.

'I mean… overalls – or do you call them something else?'

'It's the right thing to wear … today …'

She could be so irritatingly superior.

'Really? So what is happening today? Off to a plumber's convention?'

She swung around. Her hair hung below her shoulders, dark blonde with fair streaks from the sun. Her face was lightly tanned and the sun caught her green eyes. He saw for a moment the lovely girl he had fallen for. She used to touch him and smile. Now she wouldn't go near him and wore a determined frown. It began before she was pregnant, and seemed permanent.

'Is it really any of your business?'

'Of course it's my bloody business. You're my wife and you're what – eight months pregnant?' He felt waves of confusion passing through him as the chorus of voices started up.

One voice was saying 'You've got to control her, Cliff, you can't let women talk to you like that' (that was his father). Another was saying 'Don't get into an argument, you can't win with pregnant women' (that was his father, too, but when he wasn't drinking). Another voice chimed in. 'You shouldn't have married her, she's nothing but a slut'. (He thought that was his mother but she would never use a word like 'slut'). A little scared voice begged him please not to fight with Mummy. That one really scared him. Was it his kid, talking to him already? Or himself, hiding in the closet on those really bad nights? He didn't know who to listen to.

'At least you could remember my pregnancy dates. I'm thirty-five weeks. And why do you think being my husband gives you the right to choose my clothes and tell me where I can go?'

'Oh, give it a rest Andrea. This isn't a feminist seminar. I'm just thinking of your well-being in this heat.'

'If you must know' she said, turning back to the counter and putting layers of salad and cheese on the buttered bread with unwarranted vigour, 'I'm going to the demo.'

'What, the Vietnam War demo?'

'Yes of course the Vietnam War demo. What other demos are there?'

'Andrea! Be reasonable! They say this will be a big one – police by the truckload! Look what happened last time. Heaps were arrested. It's not safe.'

He stood behind her and put his hands on her shoulders. He meant it as a soothing gesture, but he could feel the muscles tighten and to his surprise he started gripping her firmly. He realised he wanted to shake sense into her.

'Get away from me' she said, without turning around. 'If you keep on touching me like that you'll be sorry!'

He had no doubt he would be sorry. His arms fell to his sides. He turned away and walked back to his chair.

'You know I agree with you about Vietnam. I went to the demos myself'.

'But you're not going now that it's getting heavy, are you? The pigs are going for us. Premier bloody Askin is egging them on. We must stand together and show them that they can't silence us. So what do you do? Go off to work in your white shirt! You're a crypto-fascist, Cliff, you just covered it up for a long time. But truth will out'.

Cliff slumped in his chair. He picked up his teacup and drained it. What could he do? He was sick and tired of this eternal argument. He thought of all the things he wanted to say, to get her to back off. But she knew them all and it made no difference. At his father's birthday lunch in Newcastle she told them all she was so pleased that they were solid working-class people doing their best in the face of capitalist exploitation. The whole clan heard it. His father said nothing. His mother frowned. His Uncle Sid laughed and downed his Newcastle Bitter. 'There you go, girlie' he said, 'stick it right up them!'

'Sid, please,' said Marian. She could see Sid liked Andrea.

Marian wouldn't let it go.

'We're very proud of Cliff' she said. She looked out the window, addressing the hedge of hydrangeas. 'He's really made something of himself. First in the family to go to Uni. And now he's in Law. You should be grateful'.

Andrea laughed. 'Maybe he should be grateful. I work full-time you know. And I don't support the ruling class'.

Andrea would deliver little lectures about the ruling class at the drop of a hat. He didn't know where she got this stuff. She talked like a sociologist, but in fact she had gone to the Early Childhood Education College and was employed as a kindergarten teacher in a local pre-school. She was passionate about what she called 'alternative education'. She brought home a stream of weighty books on child development.

Over pudding Brenda, Cliff's sister-in-law, bragged about the fact that her kid Jackie came first in arithmetic.

'That's nothing to be proud of' exclaimed Andrea, leaning back on the hand-carved wooden chair, one of his dad's finest pieces.

'I don't support the way bourgeois society inculcates its values into young children. Reading, writing and arithmetic are designed by capitalist society to prevent the spontaneous encounter with the world. Free children should not have to learn arithmetic!'

Brenda gasped and Cliff's mother shut her eyes, pretending she hadn't heard.

Cliff had excelled at mathematics and found this proposition ridiculous. Humans had lived for centuries without reading, writing and arithmetic, and all that meant was that they were barbarians. Without these skills there could be no accounting and no way of knowing what anybody actually owned or had borrowed.

In a way he couldn't explain Cliff felt that the ability to

account for things accurately was essentially about justice. Otherwise there was no basis for a system of law. When he tried this argument with Andrea the first time, she didn't really have an answer. She must have discussed it with someone else, though, because the next time it came up she told him that law itself was just a means of propping up the inherent inequalities in capitalism.

Cliff sometimes found her statements thought-provoking. He had studied history as part of his degree. There was no denying that ordinary people lost their common property to a limited group who got more and more wealthy as a result. It was the same in Ireland and in Australia it was even more blatant. They just took the land off the Aborigines on the grounds that they never used it properly and left them with nothing. Even now he was dealing with developers who wanted prime seafront Aboriginal reserve changed to private property with individual title.

Still, he was doing well. He liked the secure income, and the bonuses that came his way. If only Andrea would stop destroying his confidence, carrying on about 'men' all the time. Mainly he blamed the consciousness-raising group she had been attending. He felt quite easy about condemning US aggression against the peasants of Vietnam, but it was much harder to condemn all men because they occupied superior social positions due to their possession of a particular kind of genital organ.

The Phallocracy, she called it. Sometimes he allowed himself to see it from her point of view. It was true that men seemed to control everything of value, including women, simply because they were men. But what was the alternative? If they weren't men, what would they be? Or should they not exist at all?

It turned out that some feminists did think that was a good idea. Women would join together to create an egalitarian, communal way of life, raising each other's children in natural ways, which apparently included breast-feeding them until they were five, or ten, or worse, while men would be kept as stud animals in farms, their sperm milked on demand. He started reading a novel describing such a society, but he couldn't get past the first chapter.

Then there was the possibility that they were all lesbians. His mate Duncan who used to play bass in the band swore that the whole feminist business was a plot by lesbians to get straight women away from men. He said lesbians had manuals describing how to seduce married women and get them and their children into their damned communes. Was Andrea a lesbian? How would he know? She certainly looked like one in her boiler suit. Was some devious lesbian feeding her all this bullshit about men and patriarchy? If so, what could he do about it?

So many thoughts were rushing through his mind at the same time. He groaned. Andrea noticed nothing. She never did.

She had finished with his lunch and put it in the brown-paper bag. Glancing at her sideways Cliff suddenly pictured her in bed with another woman. Had she already tried it and liked it? Oh my God! Maybe he should ask her, but not this morning. This morning he had to go to work and wanted to come home to some peace and quiet. Maybe he could get in a surf before dinner. Although if Andrea was at the demo there probably wouldn't be any dinner. He willed himself to subside. Looking at her marching towards him brandishing the lunch bag did the trick.

'Okay' he said at last, 'Whatever you want. Just be careful. If it gets rough, promise me you'll keep out of the way'.

She softened. 'I will, I promise. But I can't be out of the way. I'm carrying the banner for 'Mothers United Against Imperialist Aggression'. The pregnant women are up just behind the banner, then all the women with babies in prams and strollers. Then the ones with the pre-schoolers. Half our pre-school is going to be there. The pigs won't attack us if we all stay together. They wouldn't dare! We'll be filming the whole thing. If they try anything the whole world will see'.

Her eyes were bright, and energy was sparking out from her hair. It was the sunlight shining directly in through the side window of the apartment, but just for that moment she seemed lit up like some movie Amazon, flooded with strength and power.

Cliff felt small, unimportant. He went over and gave her a polite kiss on the cheek, a little hug. He put the brown paper bag and an apple in his briefcase and looked at the clock. It was 8.30. It would be okay to go now. He called 'Bye' as he went out the door, which banged behind him, and then the music started: she was playing The Wailers' 'Get Up Stand Up' at full volume. The women all loved Bob Marley for some reason.

Cliff got into his beloved EH Holden, wincing at the sight of the new scratches which somehow appeared all the time. Kids with coins? Other drivers banging into the side of the car while parking? No matter how often he fixed them the small dents and scratches seemed to reappear. He put the car in first and drove off up Bronte Rd towards the Junction. It was only a short way, but he wasn't going to walk it in this weather.

He caught a glimpse of the blue ocean, and wished he could turn around towards the city, cross the Harbour Bridge and drive up the coast somewhere, get rid of the shirt and the suit and the brown paper bag, shoot through. Where was it men went? Mount Isa, that would do. But as soon as this thought arose, he felt deeply ashamed. He was a married man. His wife was about to have his baby. He had responsibilities. He couldn't disappoint his parents. And it was far too hot in Mt Isa, he couldn't work in a mine. On balance, he had a lot to be grateful for. Maybe it would be better when the baby came. He arrived at work with a tiny flicker of hope in his heart.

Ceiling fans pushed the hot air around. The boss's desk overlooked rooftops to the blue sea and his windows opened so he got the afternoon breeze, if there was one. When they converted the old warehouse into cubicles they had forgotten about summer in Sydney.

On Fridays they were allowed to ditch their coats and ties before the midday briefing. Then there would be lunch at a local pub. If Moriarty carried on they were meant to do the same. Cliff found himself looking forward to it even if it did mean too many beers and too much sucking up. He never drank so much that he wouldn't be home on time and Andrea said she didn't mind as long as he wasn't late for dinner, although she managed to let him know that she did mind, so he didn't do it too often. He didn't dare tell her that he hated the dinners she was cooking these days. Lentils!

ANDREA WAS SUPPOSED to meet the other women in Belmore Park at nine-thirty. But the traffic was heavy and her bus hardly moved. There were no empty seats. When she clambered aboard a young man stood up and offered her one but she declined. Now, hanging onto the strap as the bus jerked along, she regretted it. It was packed and she felt dizzy. Something seemed to be pressing up against her back, probably a bag or package, but it felt very strange. Ten minutes passed; finally, the driver opened the doors and people piled out and set off walking down the hill towards Central. Andrea was pushed off the bus and went along with it, although she would have preferred to sit down for a bit.

She stopped and leaned on a tree trunk. The leafy canopy dappled the grass. Her feet seemed strangely far away, and she realised she wasn't breathing properly. She felt pressure on her back again.

It was hot, she was tired, she hadn't slept well, it was nothing to worry about. She was determined not to give in to mere physical feelings, would not indulge herself by feeling peculiar. She had a mission, she and thousands of others, to save innocent women and children being tortured and sizzled by napalm even as she stood here under a tree on a bright Sydney morning. The odd feeling subsided and she was ready to move off with the tide of people sweeping down the hill.

Because the strategists wanted the Women's Collectives to go first they planned for the front of the march to head off early and the others to come in behind them at staggered intervals. The Revolutionary Socialist Collective, Workers for Peace and Justice, Vietnam Vets against the War and all the rest had been asked to arrive at different times so that there was space for all.

The energy was amazing. There were thousands of people already spilling over the edges of the little park and trailing round the corner and over the road. The banners stuck in the ground were the only way to find your own group. The pack of people meant the buses had all been diverted away from Central and she along with hundreds of others were walking along the road towards the park. There was excitement, tension and thrill in the air.

Some were wearing headbands and military jackets. They passed out leaflets and flyers along the way. Near the park she could hear the loudspeakers calling groups into formation, telling people to stay calm, holding them back so the women could get organised at the front.

Finally she saw Marlene and the others. A place had been cleared where the women with babies and children in strollers could line up. There were scores of them. Her group was to be right at the very front of the march. She wasn't sure how that had happened, but Marlene seemed to have a lot of influence with the organisers. She was pregnant too, but it hardly showed. She ran over and hugged her.

'Careful' said Andrea, feeling the pressure on her belly.

'Sorry' said Marlene, 'Just so happy you made it!'

'I'm glad too' said Andrea, but she was feeling strange again. 'I need some water'.

'Didn't you bring some?' asked Marlene.

'Yes, of course' said Andrea, pulling out her bottle from a string bag, 'but there isn't much left'.

'I'll see if someone has any spare'. She turned away, a bit crossly Andrea thought. She should have brought more. Marlene came back with a full bottle.

'You'll have to make that last' she said sternly. Andrea took a small sip and obediently followed her over to where the rest of the group was forming up. Several of the toddlers were crying. Andrea looked down at one of them.

'He's tired' said Amy, 'Really it's his nap time'. She pulled a biscuit out of her trouser pocket and gave it to the red-faced child, who obediently stuck it in his mouth.

There were marshals striding along towards them.

'Come on, come on' called Marlene, and handed Andrea one end of a banner reading 'We Demand Justice for the Unborn'.

Under her white overalls her T-shirt said 'Women United will Never be Defeated' and she wore countless badges: 'Women against War', 'Down with US Aggression', 'Free Vietnam', 'End Patriarchy Now'. With her short black curls and big brown eyes she looked like an angry little sprite.

Andrea felt something powerful inside her. The baby must be kicking or turning around or something. The sensation seemed to go on for ages. It was hard to think that it was a real baby already, one which would cry and suck her breasts. All around her were women, babies, children, pregnant bellies, banners, cries, shouts, loud-speakers barking out commands in the background, people reading the leaflets being thrust into their hands.

She wanted to sit down. But there was nowhere to sit – only over on the far wall, and she was carrying the banner, so it was too late.

She put her hand into a pocket and pulled out a black patterned kerchief with a red band at the end. It was her Ho Chi Minh scarf. She particularly treasured it: you could see those tiny Viet Cong guerrilla women all wearing exactly the same scarf in the newsreels. But that was usually because they had been captured and were about to be interrogated and tortured, probably raped as well. She had been given the scarf by someone who knew a vet – now a member of Vets Against the War – who had brought it back. She hoped nothing horrible had happened to its original owner. She wrapped it round her neck. It was a scratchy kind of cotton. They had to make everything themselves, so it was hand-woven, and not so comfortable to wear.

Suddenly they were being lined up and their group organiser was moving alongside with his loudhailer.

'To the front, to the front' he called, leading them on. And then they were moving out across the road towards George Street, down which they would march in formation until they reached the Town Hall. It wasn't all that far, but there was a hill down and then a hill up again.

She looked back at the women with strollers and prams behind her. The sun shone right into the babies' faces. Some wore sun hats, but others had no protection. Mothers were pulling spare nappies or wraps over them. There was a plan for emergencies, a way would be kept clear along one footpath. Men were patrolling along, trying to keep a clear space, but more people poured in from side streets and laneways and joined the throng.

At first Marlene and Andrea were right at the front leading their group, but soon others crowded in alongside. Now there were both men and women at the front of the march and the noise was deafening.

They managed to get down to Hay Street although she could hear an increasing chorus of howling infants behind her. The crowd was so great that she could not turn around to see what was happening and there was nothing to do but keep going. As they moved forward a dense line of blue uniforms appeared blocking the road.

Sydney came to a halt whenever the slightest thing happened in the narrow Victorian streets, let alone the main road linking Circular Quay with Central Station. Andrea and Marlene paused for a moment, exchanging a look of mixed fear, excitement and horror. Behind them the march pushed forward. The organisers tried to call a halt so the women at the front could rearrange themselves and the filmmakers could get into position. But the crowd stretched all the way back to Belmore Park and was still growing as more and more people arrived from the trains and buses. It had a life of its own.

The heat and noise seemed to redouble as the line of police up ahead came closer. Somebody nearby started chanting anti-police slogans, even though the organisers had begged people not to. Andrea felt her legs moving forward as the distant line of blue began to resolve itself into actual figures, then into figures carrying batons and shields.

Suddenly she felt a rush of fluid running down her legs. She had wet her pants. But she couldn't understand it because she didn't feel afraid, more rage and fury that the State would send out hundreds of uniformed police against defenceless pregnant women and children. Would rage make you wet your pants?

The march organisers moved together and linked arms across the road ahead of the women. She heard the men shouting to each other: link up, link up, slow down, some of the fleeter ones running back through the crowd trying to stop the press of people behind. Nobody had expected the police to block the road like this.

There would be a face-to-face confrontation. Surely they would not beat women and children with their batons? But then again, the violence had been getting more and more extreme and the publicity describing them as traitors, communists and deviants wasn't likely to calm the police response.

Andrea, during this slight pause, found she had stopped breathing again. And there was a growing feeling in her body. She knew she should sit down, but there was nowhere to sit. There was a loud sound coming from up ahead, and then, from a side street, a line of police on horseback clattered through into George Street and stood in front of the police lines. Several uniformed men appeared with loudhailers.

The whole march stopped a short way away from the police. The horses were restless; they didn't want to stand still and one or two were dancing around and had to be reined in. Everything went silent.

Far behind, she could still hear the marchers shouting slogans. A voice came towards them, distorted but easily understood.

'This is an illegal march' it said. 'The police will let the women and children pass only. All women and children should move forward at once and then leave as quickly as possible. All others should disperse immediately'.

'What will we do?' the women asked.

'We can't let them get away with it! We must hold together'. Mutterings and shuffling on all sides. From behind, a chant: 'The people, united, will never be defeated'. But near the front, everyone could see what lay ahead, and kept quiet. Even the kids had stopped crying. Then into the eerie silence came a wail, echoing off the old Victorian buildings lining this part of the city.

To her utter astonishment, Andrea realised the sound was coming from her own mouth. She couldn't do anything to stop it; it was purely animal. She doubled over and felt agonising pain sweep through her body.

'Oh my god, Andrea, are you all right?' Marlene rushed over.

But she could not speak, she just stood there doubled over. Then her legs gave way, and she crumpled to the ground.

'Medic, medic' called Marlene. But the medics, if there were any, weren't near the front of the march.

'We have to get you off the road', she said. Several other pregnant women broke away and half-dragged, half-carried her to the side. But there was no room on the footpath either, people were everywhere. They tried to make way, but the pressure of bodies was enormous. Suddenly the pain went away again.

'I'm OK, I'm OK, don't worry, I'll be fine. I'll just stay over here for a bit'. She had reached a building and leaned against it. 'You go on'. Marlene looked at her a moment.

'You don't think you are in labour or anything, do you?' she asked, suddenly registering the wet trousers.

'No, it can't be that' she said, 'It's not due for four weeks.'

Marlene looked at her doubtfully. Although she supported the rights of mothers she was not yet one herself and didn't know much about it.

'Well, if you're sure' she said, and turned, leaving Andrea leaning against a little shop front, beside an alcove. She watched Marlene go, feeling suddenly terribly alone and, and moments later she felt another pain gripping her, and slid to the ground. As the pain grew, spreading from her back to her front and down her legs, the same wailing sound came out of her mouth. But now no-one could hear her, because the march had suddenly lurched forward again, and the women and children and babies were all going up the road towards the line of police and horses, shouting and chanting at the top of their voices. The babies started howling again and Andrea's cries just added to the cacophony.

She did not know what to do. She felt she could stand up, if someone would help her, but the people were all marching off up the road focusing on the line of horses and police. They were still shouting at them through the loudhailers to stop at once and disperse, but their voices were muffled by the bodies.

At least with the forward movement the press of people in her little alcove diminished, and she half curled up in the corner, her mind a blur. Another pain gripped her. Only then did she realise that she was, in fact, in labour, and her baby was trying to be born. She lay there, helplessly, her heart racing, panting. Suddenly a voice was in her ear, a strong arm around her shoulders.

She opened her eyes. She couldn't believe what she

was seeing: it was a policeman in uniform. 'Come along now' he said and tried to lift her to her feet. But she bent over again with an enormous pain and screamed.

'We have to get you to hospital' he said. 'Here, try standing'. But she couldn't and crumpled to the ground and lay panting and howling. He put his jacket under her head and squatted down beside her.

'How did you find me?' she said.

'Someone said there was a woman in trouble so I came to look. I'm trained in first aid. I'm Tony. You really shouldn't be here.'

She began to think 'typical man', but the pain took her again. She heard him telling her 'Pant, pant' as she gripped his hand. Next thing, he was talking into the two-way radio. 'Emergency, emergency, get an ambulance here at once, west side of George St, this woman's about to give birth'.

Suddenly she heard a bedlam of screaming and yelling coming down the street. 'What's happened, what's happening?' she asked.

'We let the women and children through, but the rest wouldn't go back. There's a bit of a scuffle'.

But Andrea didn't care. All she could think of were the pains. The gaps between them were too short. She had to get her clothes off. She began scrabbling at the clips on her overalls. 'Help me, help me' she cried. The policeman looked up and saw a middle-aged woman still marching forward up the street. 'Here, you' he said, and grabbed her arm.

'You get off me, you pig!' she cried in outrage.

'No, please, I need your help, there's a woman here giving birth'.

'What?' cried the woman. As soon as she saw Andrea she understood.

'You're in luck. I'm a midwife. Go and get some clean cloths from somewhere, she can't just have it on the pavement'. Suddenly there were other people clustered around her, and she felt the woman's hand gripping her own. 'I'm Elspeth' she said, 'You'll be fine. How far apart are the pains?'

But another one gripped her. Elspeth helped spread something underneath her, and someone had a loose sarong and held it up in front to give her some privacy. She had to get the boiler suit off. The buckles were stuck fast. Andrea bellowed and scrabbled but nothing would move.

'Scissors, a knife, something' Elspeth called out. A woman delved in her shoulder bag and pulled out some nail scissors. Clipping through the fabric she was finally able to pull the garment down.

Another policeman appeared. 'The ambulance can't get through. There are a lot of injuries, they're trying to get them out through Park Street'.

'OK' said Tony. 'Can you keep the gawpers away? We have a midwife here'.

The second policeman stood in the alcove screening the little group with his uniform jacket as best he could, telling people to get out of the way. Mostly they did, but suddenly a man with a large camera appeared. Flashbulbs went off. 'Get out of here' said Tony, 'Can't you see this woman's having a baby!'

'Yeah, great story! What's your name, love?'

The second policeman pushed him out of the way and

tried to grab the camera, but the flash bulbs were still going off as he left.

'Bastards' said Tony, 'Utter bastards'. But Andrea didn't care. She didn't care who did or said anything because now she lived only within her own place, a place where nothing existed but herself and her own body and its rhythm of pains and release.

Someone brought water and wet towels. Elspeth was mopping her face, sweat was pouring off her. Time seemed to stop, then start again. Sirens wailed from every direction. She had no idea how long it had been going on, but the bright sun seemed to have moved along and although there were still people walking up the street the press of people had stopped and the noise had died down.

She could hear more sirens approaching. A moment later paramedics arrived with a stretcher.

'OK, we'll take it from here'.

'No, don't move her,' said Elspeth. 'I'm a midwife. I think she's almost there'.

Andrea let out another loud scream.

'Push, push'! Then, 'that's enough, wait, wait. That's it, it's crowning'.

The ambulance men stood by. Andrea felt an enormous pain gripping her body.

'That's it, push, push' Andrea felt one more great urge overcome her, and now she had to push as the greatest pain of all seized her. She pushed. Another slithery hot feeling, and the pain suddenly subsided. She panted in relief, and then heard Elspeth say, 'It's a girl!'

Andrea lay back. She couldn't believe what had happened. The ambulance men had clean cloths and were wrapping the baby. 'The placenta may take a while,' said Elspeth.

'We'll put her in the ambulance now. The hospital is standing by'.

Someone was putting cloths between her legs. She looked at the bundle in Martha's arms. 'Is she all right?' she asked.

'Perfect' said Martha, 'As perfect as a baby could be, even if she was born on George Street'.

Andrea sank back as she felt the stretcher beneath her. She felt an enormous rush of something much greater than mere happiness. She had a daughter. And she had had what was definitely a natural birth, so that was an achievement! She'd be able to tell the others in her group what a totally amazing experience it had been. No drugs at all, and no doctors. As she was put into the ambulance, she saw Elspeth's kindly face, and Tony's strong features beaming at her.

'Thank you both so much' she said, 'thank you'.

'It's OK,' said Tony. 'Take good care of the bub'. He turned away, and Andrea thought she saw tears in his eyes. Elspeth smiled at her as she passed the baby into the arms of the ambulance officer. She had blood and fluids all over her clothes. 'What will you call her?' she asked.

'Georgia. Yes, I think Georgia'. She leaned back in the ambulance, the pink baby in a transparent cradle alongside as the noise faded away behind them. She was suffused with a deep sense of satisfaction.

～

CLIFF FOUND himself sitting at an open-air bar in seaside Coogee. Jamie had driven him there in his brand-new orange HJ Monaro GTS coupe. Cliff was dizzy with envy.

Jamie was a client, a real operator. He had come into the office with some documents for signature and Moriarty had insisted he come to lunch. He had been buying up old cottages near Bronte Beach and proposed to demolish them for a major apartment complex. Moriarty was helping him with the Council permissions.

Jamie was not the kind of man Cliff normally spent time with. He was flash and wore a diamond signet ring. His linen jacket was tastefully crumpled. The low-cut collar of his white shirt revealed a gold chain around his neck, nestled into shiny chest hair. Cliff thought he should dislike him, loathe him even, with his curls and white smile. But instead, he felt drawn to him as if Jamie had some magnetic quality. There was an elegance to his well-muscled body, he moved like a dancer.

They left the office in an ebullient mood. On the way out Cliff binned his sandwiches. Something good was going down. Jamie unlocked the car and Cliff slung himself into the passenger's seat inhaling that intoxicating new vehicle smell. They drove ahead of the others down the hill towards an ocean fizzing with light. The pub was a nice place, tasteful, with potted palms and sea-breezes. Soon they were all around a table, laughing and joking. Moriarty downed designer beers and the office girls flirted and drank white wine. They ate fish and chips and pizza and salad and started on tiramisu and coffee.

Cliff sat next to Jamie and they fell into an intense conversation. When everyone got up to leave Jamie asked him if he wanted to kick on for a bit. Cliff knew it was a bad idea. He knew he should go back to the office and pick up his papers and put them in his briefcase and drink some coffee and get his head straight and drive home before he had a burning hangover from the junk food and booze in the heat.

But there was something in him today. Something about the warm salty sea air and the sprinkle of clouds and the bright blue sky and the talk and the feeling of being close to Jamie, who seemed to be listening to him, hearing him, and it was something he craved, had been craving for ever maybe, he was being recognised. Jamie seemed to see the unique person who dwelled inside his obedient exterior, he had seen through his disguise as an ordinary man, a man about to be a father. A husband. Andrea's husband. Oh God. He suddenly realised he did not want to be Andrea's husband any more. That was a definite fact.

Jamie was talking to him. The white teeth appeared and disappeared as he smiled, grinned, uttering words Cliff couldn't quite hear. The afternoon tide swelled, voices rose from the beach and people laughed in the pretty bar with its hanging ferns and swaying palms. But these were not the noises that stopped him from hearing Jamie. It was his own internal monologue filling his mind with a kind of urgent buzzing. He knew he was smiling stupidly and could feel the muscles in his cheeks going into spasms. He couldn't stop watching Jamie's face, the shadows flickering over his fine cheekbones, and he thought he asked Jamie if they could go out together tonight, or tomorrow, or both, although he wasn't sure if he really said this, or just wanted to.

But it was getting towards evening and Jamie suddenly

stood and picked up his linen jacket from the back of the chair.

'Well old sport it's been great, but I've got to get home for dinner.'

Suddenly Cliff realised he had not asked Jamie about his family. He should have asked. But being with Jamie was like being with a wizard, or a magician, or a superior being. You don't ask whether a person like that has a family. And yet he needed to know.

'Do you have kids?'

Jamie laughed.

'Hardly. I don't think children are for me. They wouldn't fit into my lifestyle'.

This was a remarkable idea. How could you decide about something like that? Surely children just came along when you had a woman. It was true that these days there was that Pill, women didn't have to get pregnant. And abortion. But that was a last resort. How could you decide to abort your own baby? He couldn't imagine it.

Then again, did Jamie even have a woman?

Cliff was standing up. Things seemed a little unstable, as though the world had gone out of focus. Jamie had taken his hand but instead of shaking it he was holding it palm up, pressing it gently with his other hand: a palm sandwich.

'We'll see each other again soon, I'm sure'.

He stared at their hands, two darkly tanned, one pale and freckled.

'Yes. I hope so. We will won't we?'

Cliff felt he should take his hand back but somehow couldn't. Jamie smiled, a strange, almost triumphant smile, and broke the connection.

'Can I give you a lift? Back to the office?'

'Yes, OK, yes, thanks'.

And he felt himself almost scuttling along to the laneway where the lurid orange car was tucked into a spot under the trees. Jamie had been drinking steadily all afternoon, but he seemed no worse for wear. He drove along the narrow road and up the hill, towards the setting sun. Cliff tried to talk but the words didn't come out. He was looking at Jamie's profile, wanting something from him. But what? The touch on his hand seemed to burn.

Jamie turned on the radio a few minutes away from the Junction. The newsreader's voice said, 'scenes of chaos along George Street' and went on to describe the lines of police, the marchers, the confrontation. And then added, almost as an aside, 'As police and demonstrators clashed a woman gave birth on the pavement near Cecil Lane. She was assisted by police and a midwife before being taken to hospital. Both mother and baby are doing well'.

Cliff heard the words blankly. Surely it wasn't possible. It couldn't be. There must have been plenty of pregnant women at the demo, it wasn't necessarily Andrea giving birth in public in the middle of town. But if it was her! Where was she? He wanted to explain the situation to Jamie but he felt so ashamed. How could he have spent the afternoon drinking and laughing with a stranger while his own baby was being born on a dirty city pavement? What kind of a man would do that?

So he said nothing. He waved goodbye with a bright smile and a cheery wave, retrieved his car from the office garage and sped home. He had to shower, change his clothes, which smelled of beer and cigarettes. Then –

what? – ring the police? Andrea's mother? (Groan!). His mind was not processing properly.

He got in the door of the flat and the phone was ringing. He picked up. It was King George Hospital, and a crisp voice told him they had been trying to contact him. He was a father, his wife had had a baby girl, everything was fine. He thought he should make some kind of excuse, but that would be pointless. The voice gave him a ward number and told him visiting hours started in an hour but if he got there earlier they would make an exception.

He hardly had time to take his jacket off before the phone was ringing again. It was Andrea's mother. Her voice was cool. He wanted her to shut up and leave him alone, but he had to be polite. He was muttering excuses – a work thing, a meeting, couldn't get back, had no idea what was happening – it sounded feeble.

He threw himself into a hot shower and scrubbed his skin and hair, his teeth and tongue. He supposed he would have to kiss Andrea. And there would be a baby, his baby. Would he see it? Would he hold it? Did he want to? He dressed in slacks and a long-sleeved shirt. Would that be the right thing to wear to a women's hospital? He had no idea.

The cab struggled through the Friday evening traffic but Cliff didn't mind. He wanted to get out near Central Station and catch a train to anywhere, anywhere at all, Broken Hill or Brisbane or some blighted desert town. At the hospital he paid the driver and went up in the lift.

Andrea was propped up on pillows in a corner bed. The last rays of the sun reflected across the room and picked up every strand of her shining hair. In her arms lay a tightly wrapped bundle. Her hospital gown was open at the front, a swollen, blue-veined breast with its vast pink centre glaring at him.

Her gaze was completely focused on the sleeping baby. When she realised it was Cliff hovering at the edge of the bed she smiled. Then frowned. Then looked down. Then looked up again.

'So you managed to get here, did you?'

Cliff just stared at her. He didn't know what to say.

'Are you … is it? … are you … the baby …. OK?'

'Yes, Georgia and I are quite OK. Thanks for asking. Where have you been?'

He didn't know what to say. He started to mutter something about work, but a single cold look stopped him.

'They called you at work. Six times. And at home. What the hell has been going on?'

Cliff stared at her. What to say? Was it his fault that she had gone out against his wishes? She was the one who had decided to do something crazy and dangerous, to take her unborn baby out into the scary world to parade around with her feminist friends and make a public spectacle of herself. He felt currents of anger and firmed up his jaw. She must have seen it because she looked away.

Suddenly she tightened the blanket around the baby and lifted her towards him.

'Don't you want to meet your daughter?'

Cliff leaned forward and took the bundle awkwardly. As he held the little body close to his chest the small face twitched, and her deep blue eyes opened. She seemed to be looking directly into him.

He felt a rush of something and suddenly there were

tears in his eyes. He looked up at Andrea and there was an astonishing understanding between them.

'She's lovely' he said. He leaned down and kissed the soft pink forehead and drank in the strangely compelling baby scent.

A nurse appeared in the room.

'Well, Daddy turned up after all'.

She bustled around briskly, propping Andrea higher in the bed.

'Come along now Mum, try her on the breast again. It's important that she takes the colostrum. Protective, you know'.

Andrea took the baby and re-adjusted her breast, struggling to get it into the baby's mouth. Cliff looked away.

He supposed he should say something more. Apologies were usually a good idea with Andrea, and he started working out how best he could express his abjection when he remembered how it felt, drinking with Jamie by the seaside. Why should he have to apologise for that? Why should a quiet drink with a mate cause such a drama? What right did she have to make him feel this bad? He felt a deep change come over him. He was determined not to let her get away with it. He was his own man.

But then he saw the little face, the tiny hand which had wound itself so trustingly around his finger. Whatever happened, that little baby was his daughter and he felt what could only be love.

He leaned down and kissed Andrea's slightly damp forehead.

'I'm sorry I wasn't with you for the birth' he said. 'But you did brilliantly on your own'.

'I wasn't really alone' she said. 'I had other women to support me'. She forgot to mention the policeman. It had been a bit embarrassing, out on the street like that. Still, she had had a short labour and completely natural childbirth so that showed what kind of a woman she was. She took a quick look at Cliff, at his stiff face, his strangely blank eyes, almost defiant. He just didn't get it. Oh well. It didn't matter what he thought. She was a new woman, a woman for new times. And this little bundle at her breast was her revolutionary baby.

3

———

DANGEROUS HONOURS

November is a beautiful time on the Birchgrove waterfront. The jacarandas burst into purple. Flocks of lorikeets shriek and feed from the honeyed gums lining the parkland. Simone should not have been drinking the night before.

Music from the forties played somewhere in the old weatherboard house. Undoubtedly Inch or one of his pals had put it on. He always had someone staying, an endless parade of single men, grizzled, down-at-heel, well past middle age, semi-alcoholics. A few were locals, they came round and drank beer and argued until they passed out. Some were strangers. Simone was more and more uncomfortable at the sight of them lounging on the veranda, stinking up the toilets, helping themselves to tea and coffee and anything else that happened to be in the main kitchen. She constantly thought about how to get rid of Inch but couldn't bear to think of the consequences. Christine said she could not make him leave, he was Simone's father's mate since forever.

Simone's part of the house was the "flatette": one room with a bed and chairs and a sofa and desk, a tiny kitchen off the hallway and her own bathroom. There was no bath, only a shower over a grate in the tiles, but at least she could keep it scrubbed clean and everyone else out of it.

One of the most powerful legacies of growing up in Paris was her visceral hatred of dirty bathrooms. Half the places they had lived in didn't even have bathrooms; people washed in deep porcelain sinks in the corner of the kitchen. If there were bathrooms they were invariably grubby, the tiles cracked, faded curtains half closed over dirty windows, and there was a penetrating smell which never quite went away, no matter how much effort went into cleaning. It was something to do with the drains in the 5th Arrondissement, or so Serge, her mother's boyfriend, said.

She turned on the tepid water and soaped her body. She was so pale. She had tried the beach a few times but the heat was overwhelming. How people could lie all day stretched out on the baking sand was beyond her. She didn't tan, there was no point in trying. Towelling herself dry she looked at the alarm clock on her desk and flinched. Late!

She couldn't be late for the seminar. She MUST NOT be late for the seminar. Normally the Third Year Honours students weren't even allowed to go to the seminar, which was strictly for Fourth Year Honours students and post-graduates. But this year was different. Everything was different. The new Head had decided that next year's Honours applicants would attend. Her friend Meredith thought they were meant to say something, speak up, make a comment, participate. Unheard of at the old Department.

Simone had already decided to wear her black pants and a long-sleeved shirt. She didn't want to look too casual, but at the same time she wasn't going to get dressed up and look ridiculous. She dried herself quickly and started to dress. The pants were very tight. They must have shrunk in the wash.

Someone knocked.

'Simone, are you awake? Aren't you going to Uni today?'

It was Christine, her … what? Stepmother? Foster mother? Father's girlfriend? Landlady? Reluctant, she opened the door.

'Christine, yes, I'm up, I'm getting dressed'.

'Those pants …!'

They clung to her fine frame like a second skin.

'You should wear a dress over them'.

'Mmm. I'm going to wear my red shirt'.

'I suppose that's long enough. What time do you have to be there?'

'It starts at two. But it's at the new campus, remember I told you the Department is moving?'

'I thought that was for next year.'

'Yes, well this is a kind of trial run. I must get a bus, I wrote the number down somewhere, it goes all the way out of the city'.

'I'd offer to drive you but the car is in the garage, something's wrong with the starter motor'.

"Oh don't worry, thanks, another time'.

'You know what I'm going to say'.

'Yes, yes, I know, I need to get my license'.

It was a sore point. Christine wanted Simone to get her license so she didn't feel obliged to drive her. And if she had her licence Simone could drive Christine. Christine was an artist. She painted abstracts in lurid neon tones. Her left eye needed an operation but she was too afraid to do it in case she lost her sight altogether. If Simone could drive it would save her so much worry.

'When will you be back?'

'I don't know. Don't expect me or anything'.

'No, fine, but phone if you're going to be very late. I can't help worrying. You don't know your way around out there, beyond the city ....' Christine had followed her out of the house, still talking a mile a minute.

'And I forgot to tell you, the plumbers have to come again, the drains aren't working properly, maybe it's the tree roots, I haven't really got time to ring them up, I do wish you were home a bit more'.

Simone muttered under her breath 'As if ...'.

'What was that?'

'Nothing, nothing, honestly I will try but I have to finish all this translation work'.

Christine nodded. 'Yes, yes, I know, I'm sorry, but it's just so hard, I can't seem to get on top of everything'. Simone's work was the only thing keeping regular money coming in which helped with the groceries and expenses but it was so inconvenient.

'Oh, and I forgot, this came for you in the mail.'

She handed her a large manila envelope with a university logo. They were always sending things in the mail, reminders, surveys, demands for information. She shoved it in her briefcase and ran up the street. It was an affectation, that briefcase, but it had been her father's. His initials, EBF, were etched in gold on the front flap. It was one of the only things he left her. Inexplicably he had left the house to Christine.

Christine had no children of her own, and tried to mother Simone, but Simone did not want to be Christine's daughter. There was a gap at her centre where a mother should have been but she had papered it over and filled it in with cement so there was no space for Christine, even if she had been a different kind of person, but she wasn't, she was a daffy hippy who had no idea what was really going on and had been sponging off Edgar for years. Christine as her mother? No thanks. Although she might have been better than Sylvie, her "real" mother. Whatever that meant.

In 1968 Simone was almost fifteen. Sylvie sent her back from Paris to stay with her father even though he was even then drinking far too much and in no fit state to care for a teenage girl. But Sylvie had to stay in Paris with Serge. To support him was her role in history, she said. Admittedly she was drunk at the time. In early 1974 Serge abandoned Sylvie. He said he was going to Italy to join the Red Brigades. She slunk back to Sydney and asked if she could move into the Birchgrove house. Edgar welcomed her and Christine didn't seem to mind. Simone was outraged and refused to speak to her. In the end Sylvie realised what a mess the Birchgrove situation was and moved to Melbourne. Then it turned out she had cancer. She died within the year.

Simone tried not to think about her mother, about what had happened, about Paris. Paris was seven years ago. Ever since she came back to Australia the only thing that anchored her had been this house. And her father had left it to Christine! The pain never abated, but lately she had begun to feel a kind of freedom, the possibility that it might not be a disaster if she moved out, moved on. She had her own life, her own career, and there was a chance she might qualify for a scholarship. There was no way she was going to help Christine by ringing up the Council or finding builders or plumbers or doing anything other than focus on her own work.

The bus passed through the city and into alien suburbs. Everything seemed so calm and ordered. Australia had been in turmoil for years: the anti-Vietnam war protests, women in revolt, the Labor Prime Minister sacked, but there was no sign of that here among the neat gardens and brick houses. Politics in Australia seemed pretty tepid. It didn't matter who was in power, they were old white men grandstanding to preserve their privileges. But somehow all the drama had affected the university and this in turn affected her.

She hadn't had time to eat anything and her stomach grumbled. She longed for strong coffee. She had only been to Hilltop once before, for some compulsory student orientation thing. The Head of Studies, Professor Newton, was trying to enthuse them about the new facilities, the brand-new library, the cafes and bars taking shape in the middle of what had been open space full of fruit-trees and rabbits. It was all concrete and sharp angles and weirdly shaped buildings with code names. They were ushered into a large glass space overlooking bushland and told it was New Human Sciences Second Building on the West, or NHSB2W.

Like most of the students, she hated it. She wanted a university to look like a university, not like some industrial production site. She had been around enough universities to know that they had to smell a particular way, to have narrow corridors and polished balustrades, gargoyles and statues, green lawns and dusty libraries full of old books nobody opened. Something like the Sorbonne. Hilltop University was never going to be the Sorbonne.

The bus stopped at an interchange near a railway station. Another bus went from there to the university. Simone really needed the toilet, but she didn't dare miss the shuttle for fear the next one might not come for half an hour. So she held herself in and hoped for the best.

It took twenty minutes to get to the campus and they had almost arrived when she remembered the envelope. She opened it and gasped. The incoming honours students would be required to give a five-minute talk introducing themselves, describing their proposed thesis project. All the supervisory staff would be present.

Her heart almost stopped. It was a catastrophe. It was her own fault. She should have contacted Dr Flannery after that conversation with Meredith but she couldn't, she just couldn't.

FOUR WEEKS earlier Simone had been perching uneasily on a wooden chair in the Student's Union, her briefcase at her feet.

A bundle of typed notes summarised her areas of research, but she needed to understand more about the process. Meredith had agreed to talk to her about it. Meredith was unusually well informed because her father was an academic. He was a scientist, so it wasn't quite the same, but Meredith knew things about how Australian universities worked that others did not. They were drinking weak coffee.

'Meredith, how do they decide who gets to be your supervisor?'

Meredith swung her long brown hair over her shoulder and laughed.

'Well there's all kinds of ways really. Once upon a time the brightest students sucked up to the most famous staff members so by the time they got to Fourth Year it was already decided'.

'But how did they know who was famous? And what if that supervisor didn't want to accept a student for some reason?'

'It is a kind of magic, almost invisible. The most popular supervisors have a book out based on their PhD research. The young men with the best results do their courses and get into their tutorials and write essays quoting their books and papers and criticise their critics. If they keep up High Distinction results that person will be their supervisor. And if they get First Class Honours at the end of Fourth Year then they get a postgraduate scholarship and go on to do a PhD with the same person. There might be one or two each year and together they become a kind of gang. Very competitive among themselves, but protective of their supervisor and vice versa, and it can go on like this more or less indefinitely'.

'Yes, now you've put it that way -- like all the boys doing African Studies with Dr Minchin, now they're off doing fieldwork in Botswana or somewhere. He's

Manchester school apparently. Doesn't seem to have much to do with us here in Australia'.

Simone was very sensitive to historical and cultural differences and what defined research in the social sciences. She did not want to talk about it to her fellow students because she did not want anyone to know who her mother was or that she had been in Paris in May' 68. Or that her mother was close to all the French academics who just now were beginning to be talked about in England and the US. Or that as a child she had sat on their knees sometimes and received their smoky kisses on both cheeks.

Meredith drained her coffee and lit a cigarette. 'But things are changing now, with girls coming into the university in numbers, and not just to find rich husbands'.

Simone laughed. The idea of finding a rich husband at university had never occurred to her.

'So what difference does it make? Having more girls?'

'Well you might think it makes it fairer, or more equal or something, and maybe it does for the undergraduates. But having bright girls wanting to go on to Honours and Postgraduate work upsets the system'.

'What do you mean?'

'The academic staff are mostly men. So the pretty girls, if they play their cards right, can get a supervisor who's more interested in their panties than their theses'. Simone nodded. Of course it would be like that.

'Aren't most of them married?'

'Yes but what difference does that make? Some are incorrigible. They have their pick from the new girl students every year. But it doesn't mean the girls will do well. A few might, but generally the old rules hold, only the men get First Class Honours which give a guaranteed PhD scholarship. Look at last year's class. Twelve Honours students, seven of them girls, only one got First Class and a scholarship. And that caused a lot of trouble'.

'So what are we doing here? Why are we even bothering to do Honours?'

'Well I love being at uni. I'd like to go on and make it a career. It's worth a try. I love the books and the thinking and the writing and the ideas and the seminars, the whole thing. I'd rather be doing this than anything else I can think of'.

Simone admired Meredith. She was open and honest. She trusted her, but at the same time she kept her at a distance, because if Meredith knew how Simone lived, what her family situation was like, what she had gone through in Paris with her mother, she might not understand. And it might put her off, and she might no longer want to be her friend.

'So do you have a supervisor?'

Meredith put her hand on Simone's.

'I haven't told anyone in our group yet' she said. 'But I won't be here next year. My father has got a lectureship in Tasmania. We're all moving. I know it's weird, but I'd rather stay with my family and go to University in Hobart than struggle on here on my own. Now that the Department is being split up and half the staff are moving to Hilltop there's no telling what will happen, how it will turn out. I want to work somewhere quiet and conservative. There's so much going on here I can't see how going into a brand-new system with new arrangements is going to be good for me. Dad agrees. He says the humanities in

Sydney are doomed. Mind you, he always says the humanities are doomed'.

'But he doesn't mind that you are doing them?'

'No, Mum and Dad are great, if it leads to an academic career that's good and if it doesn't they know I'll find something else, doing English and History and Social Sciences I can always be a teacher'.

'And can you get into Honours in Tasmania?'

'Well it's not official yet, but they say there'll be no problem. I'm going to switch my focus to British seafarers and early settlement, pretty much straight history, thank heavens I kept on with history as a major'.

'I'll be sorry, I'll miss you'.

'Yes, I'll be sorry too, it's been great having you as a friend. We'll keep in touch'.

They sat a while as the setting sun's rays lit up the pale blue cloud of cigarette smoke and dust motes.

'Well, anyway, I wanted to ask your advice about supervision. You know I'm going to apply for one of the new scholarships at Hilltop'.

'Yes, you said. It'd be great if you got one'.

'But I have to have a supervisor. They sent me a letter about it, they want to appoint Dr Flannery, you know, the lecturer in Social Theory'.

She hadn't officially met the woman, although she had seen her in the corridors and heard her rather abrasive voice raised in protest at something wrong in the mail-room or some omission by the Departmental Secretary who clearly didn't like Dr Flannery.

'Her? What? Why?'

'That's the thing, I don't know'.

'Who sent the letter?'

'You know, what's her name, Mrs. Betjeman. But I imagine the new Head must have decided it, she would just be sending on the letter'.

'I wouldn't be too sure. Mrs. Betjeman really runs the place, has done for years. What topic did you put down?'

'Women and exploration in the Pacific. You know I've been working on the early French explorers' journals. I want to show how the Islanders and the explorers had no idea what each side was doing, and how the local women got caught up in it then turned it to their own advantage'.

'Ha, well that's probably it. Flannery is the only one who does anything on "women", which they think is the same as feminism. If you mention women you'll get Flannery. Her PhD was something about Women in Philosophy, so it makes a kind of sense'.

'But she won't know anything about the Pacific'.

'No, and she'll tell anyone who asks that she's not a feminist, or at least not one of the current lot'.

Dr Flannery was a short strong-looking woman with straight greying hair cut in a severe bob. She never wore make-up and dressed mostly in plain slacks and loose shirts. She might have been forty, or even fifty. Her skin was clear and unwrinkled, her eyes dark and alert, as if she was constantly waiting for something to happen.

'How come she never took us in tutorials? We both did Social Theory in Second Year'.

'She doesn't take undergraduate tutorials. Apparently there were too many student complaints, she was too aggressive or unsympathetic or something. They made her give lecture courses in those second-rate subjects like Health Sciences and Social Work. Neither of the factions in the Philosophy Department would have her'.

'So what, would it be the kiss of death to have her as a supervisor?'

'Maybe. But in the new University it might be different. She's the kind of cross-disciplinary person they are supposed to want, and getting more women academics is part of their brief as well. She's pretty smart apparently'.

'Really? Who says?'

'She's just had two papers published in the English journals; it's been causing quite a stir'.

'What are they about?'

'Oh, I don't remember exactly. Something about what's wrong with the new feminist theory, not Marxist enough or it doesn't understand the working class'.

'Oh'. Simone had heard enough about what was wrong with theory to last a lifetime.

'But can they do that? Just assign me to someone without her even knowing me?'

'I think they can. It's in some rule somewhere, you'd have to look it up. Listen, take my advice, go and see Flannery, find out what she's got to say about it, if you don't want her, go and find one of the others that you think you could work with and get him onside. The thing is, they all need Honours students, it looks good on their records, and you need someone to stick up for you, argue your case for a scholarship, especially now that everything is so upside down with the re-organisation'.

She pulled her hair back again, haloed in the light.

'And she's been getting very involved with the anti-urban renewal activists, the Builder's Labourers' Federation and so on. I agree with them of course. It's disgusting that the developers are trying to destroy the whole of old Sydney and build horrible new apartments. She used to attend all the rallies and give speeches and write news sheets for them. She was a friend of that woman activist, the rich one, what's her name, Melitta Pettifer, the publisher, the one who disappeared in July?'

'Really? I thought that was all mixed up with the criminal underworld. Dr Flannery? That's amazing'. It piqued her interest. Maybe Dr Flannery would be okay after all.

'But honestly Simone, I'm not the person to ask. You really ought to make an appointment, see what she says. It's not like before, where you could change your mind even after you'd started your thesis and write something completely different, like Keira Bentley did when Dr Dragovic arrived'.

Even she had been dimly aware of the dramas around Keira and Dr Dragovic. She was considered a straight First Class Honours student thanks to the former Head of Department's support but when Dr Dragovic arrived in mid-year she dropped both thesis topic and supervisor and started working on some obscure philosopher none of them had heard of. It was rumoured that the former Head had been forced to resign after punching Dr Dragovic in the Staff Club.

Meredith lit another cigarette. At least it was something inoffensive. The smell of Paris had come through a cloud of Gauloise. Even breathing at home was hard when she was younger, with Edgar and his pals all puffing away.

'There's Dr. Dixon. He works on the Pacific, yes?'

Simone knew his name but she couldn't picture his face. He was another one new to the Department, transferred in from somewhere else where a department was being closed for lack of students. Religious Studies came to mind although she didn't think there was an actual Religious Studies department. Who knew?

'He gave a talk in History not long ago, about missionaries. He's American, that's a bit off-putting. He seemed all right but he wears ridiculous suits. At least he didn't seem to be a groper. Read his book, he must have written one or he wouldn't be in a tenured position'.

The sun had set and the lights in the café made a sickly green patina over everything.

'Sorry, Simone, but I really must go now. Mum's cooking a proper dinner tonight, my brother and his fiancée are coming over'.

'Of course, of course. And thanks so much for the advice'.

'It's not much I'm afraid. But you need to get a bit more involved. If you want to get anywhere you've got to find out who's who and what's what'.

'I'm really sorry you're going to Hobart. I hope it will be great for you. But I will miss you'.

'Don't worry, you'll make new friends, you know some already and there'll be new people coming in from the other Departments, it might even be fun! Look on the bright side!'

Simone hugged her. Meredith was always so positive and enthusiastic. That was what would carry her on into a happy life, no matter what happened: an optimistic innocence. It was endearing. People who had grown up in Australia had no idea what it was like out in the big world, the turmoil and drama going on as empires crumbled and power structures collapsed.

As far as the universities were concerned, knowledge was theirs to manage, reformulate and reproduce. They defined what it was. It grew from Empire itself. It could go on indefinitely if only silly students stopped making nuisances of themselves and acting inappropriately. And when their infantile demands became too much, one could always start a new University to corral the dissidents and make sure the valuable knowledge created over previous decades remained unchallenged. They would do whatever it took to maintain the rituals and formalities, which were what really mattered.

Simone despised herself for being right in the middle of it. She had committed to life as an academic, a scholar and researcher. Now was not the time to question why, or even to ask if there was any alternative. She felt she had been propelled in a certain direction by her past and now she faced the unknowable. She had not even thought of how she would fit in with this process, she had acted as if she could do what she liked and get away with it indefinitely. Which, in a way, had been true, up to now at least.

SHE HAD NOT MADE an appointment to see Dr Flannery, or Dr Dixon, or anyone else for that matter. She did not have a supervisor. And now she was pushing across through the hot airless campus into a concrete building with hand-drawn signs saying, "Upstairs to the Human Sciences Seminar", late, trailing after others who she could see bunched up ahead of her. Just in time she had found a block of toilets tucked away at the bottom of a set of concrete stairs. They were unisex.

People were milling around trying to work out where they should sit. Professor Newton was fussing at the top of the table while Mrs. Betjeman placed sheets of printout in front of each chair, where glasses of water and small notebooks and pencils were also laid out. Simone recognized a few students from her former classes. There seemed to be quite a few academics from English and Philosophy. She couldn't see Dr Flannery or Dr Dixon.

Soon it was apparent there were not enough chairs so Mrs. Betjeman sent a couple of students to find some from another room. Professor Newton indicated that the students sitting at the table should give up their seats to the hovering academics and sit against the back wall instead.

Simone was already as far away from the table as possible.

'I thought this was supposed to be for the students' said an intense looking boy with long dark hair and very white skin. 'Why should the academic staff get to sit at the main table?'

'Typical' said a pretty girl with pale pink lips.They were obviously together and sat down next to Simone. The girl leaned over, putting out a grubby hand with chipped nail polish.

'Hi' she said, 'I'm Derry, this is Oscar. We're new here, what about you?'

'Yes, well no, I was at the old Uni, the Metro, until they moved half of it here. Not that it's really here yet'. She laughed uneasily.

'God no, it's not is it? It's just a building site'.

'Where are you from?'

'Oh, we are – well, we were - at the Arts College. They are moving the Art History people here but not the artists. They are going to the new Technical College. There aren't any studios or anything here. So if you want to do a degree in art that actually involves painting you're out of luck'. Oscar grimaced, showing strong white teeth.

'How will that work? Don't you want to paint?'

'Yes, we do, but this looks like a good option and it's only for a year. They've offered places and a chance for one of the new Scholarships, so we thought we'd give it a try. We've been majoring in Art History anyway. The painting teachers weren't much good. Boring abstract expressionists mostly. But it means there's no real art course left in the city now'.

'God, I had no idea'.

'No, well, nobody cares about art anymore, if they ever did'.

Derry pulled out a packet of cigarettes and offered them round to the students nearby.

'Sorry, there's no smoking' said a mournful looking boy, gesturing at a red sign on the wall.

The other seats filled up and there was no more space in the room. It was stuffy, the windows only opened halfway and the ceiling fans swirled about vaguely pushing the hot air around. Some of the academic staff spoke in low voices to each other. Students at the back were chattering, complaining about the heat and the delay but not wanting to draw attention to themselves. Simone wriggled on the folding chair, wishing she had worn looser pants. She thought of chatting more to Oscar and Derry but she didn't know what to say.

Professor Newton continually popped in and out of the room and there was a strange air of expectation and excitement. Student presentations of their thesis topics usually weren't all that exciting, even if there was a competitive edge to them.

It was obvious there was a hold-up. Then the Professor burst back into the room, followed by Mrs. Betjeman wheeling some boxes on a trolly and behind her an elegantly dressed handsome man in a dark suit and impeccable white shirt. He ran his hand through abundant grey hair and there was an audible sigh in the room. He was just so good-looking, like a movie star.

Professor Newton pulled out a chair for the visitor.

"Please, here, please do sit down, make yourself comfortable, some cold-water, Mrs. Betjeman please, at once ..."

Two or three staff members had leaped to their feet and were shaking hands with the visitor enthusiastically. Others gaped.

'Is it really him?' one asked, so loudly that even Simone could hear. Her heart was beating fast, she thought it must be a hallucination. She wanted to say, 'Yes, guess what, it really is him' but of course she couldn't. She could hardly breathe. The room was alive with mutterings.

'Who? Who is it?' asked Derry. 'Do you know?'

'I don't know' said Oscar. 'Do you?' he asked, turning to Simone. 'Must be someone very important'.

Simone shook her head.

Professor Newton held his hands up, as if blessing a congregation.

'Ladies and gentlemen, students, staff, please, please, quiet please'.

The hubbub died down a little.

'So, as you can see, we have a most unexpected surprise for you. What an honour, what a great honour' he said. 'Ladies, gentlemen, scholars, please let me introduce to you a visitor to our shores, who has so generously agreed to speak to us today: Professor Jean-Pierre Daladier'. He beamed, and he began clapping his hands. Most followed suit. A few of the academic staff sat stiffly without any expression.

Newton went on. 'It was the greatest good fortune that this Seminar coincided with the flying visit of my dear colleague, who I am sure you all know by repute, or if you do not already know him, you soon will. Professor Daladier is *en route* from his visiting lectureship at Yale University where he has threatened to remake the field of the humanities from the bottom up, so to speak, and spearhead the fight for new forms of knowledge and power. He is already, through his publications and distinguished lectures in France, the leader of the revolution now happening in our fields of thought'.

More clapping.

'He doesn't look like much of a revolutionary' said Oscar. 'Just another white guy in a suit'.

'Shh' said Derry. 'God, he's very good-looking'.

Simone felt as if she were floating and might at any moment land in that alternate space and time, Paris, where the rest of the world no longer existed and she would be stranded once again with her mother, her mother's boyfriend Serge, and Daladier, young philosopher-star and her mother's occasional lover. The talking would go on day and night and never stop. Now she was dizzy with a kind of fear, the fear of being recognised, the fear of not being recognised. He was there, in the flesh, in front of her eyes. They had shared so much, so intensely, the four of them, penetrating all of Paris, travelling sometimes to another city where meetings or discussions were held, sometimes in secret. They said she was a child, but she had loved him and adored him and sometimes hated him and treasured every moment he sat with her in the weak sunshine in the courtyard and listened attentively to whatever she said.

When her mother sent her back to Sydney she was certain it was to get her away from Daladier. Simone watched her mother watching Daladier, a suspicious frown making little lines between her eyebrows. He treated Simone with the utmost courtesy and appropriate distance, no matter what she did to attract his attention to make him love her more than, or instead, of her mother. She blamed herself for still being such a child and so uneducated and still unable to speak French properly or understand even half of what he said, but she knew he at least liked her.

Now, unlikely as it seemed, he was here in Sydney, just across the room, so close she could almost smell the scent that always clung around him, North African oud. For five minutes the Professor introduced this new Daladier, older, more confident, still devastatingly handsome, finally concluding with a gesture towards the box of books now sitting on a table behind him.

'And at the end of our seminar, you will receive a copy of one of Professor Daladier's most recent books, his masterwork *L'Écriture Fauve* which he has already signed personally. It is of course in French, although I am told a translation into English is in preparation as we speak'.

He nodded at Professor Daladier, who nodded back and smiled broadly around the room.

Wow. It was a great title. "Wildcat Writing". Simone

recalled fragments of their conversations, of Daladier breathing strongly as he illustrated his points on the table.

'I thought this was supposed to be a seminar for the students" said one boy with a straggling beard clutching a large folder stuffed with papers. 'I've been working all night on my presentation'.

'Me too, me too' came murmurs from around the room.

There would be no presentations today. There would be no time, with so many students and Daladier about to start speaking. He never spoke for less than an hour. Once at the Sorbonne in front of a packed audience he had spoken non-stop for almost three. Relief flooded over her. She would be able to do what was necessary to get the scholarship. But right now she was torn. She wanted to flee, to get away from the presence of this man who gave off an allure she desperately admired. But equally she wanted to go to him, to remind him of who she was and how he had once called her his "little cabbage". She dreaded how she would feel if he did not remember her.

If only she hadn't sat so far up the back.

Then Daladier began to speak. His mellifluous voice full of dramatic pauses echoed across the room through a breathless hush. Nobody dared move, or ask a question, or interrupt. Simone knew this audience was even less capable of understanding what he was saying than most. It wasn't that his English was poor or badly expressed, or his accent too extreme, but it was what he said, and what it meant. Simone had heard some of it before, in French. Now it was in English, of a kind. He talked on enthusiastically, with gestures and facial expressions which made him look one moment like an angel, another, a devil.

Finally Professor Newton had to interrupt the flow.

'I am so very sorry, Professor Daladier, but we have long passed the time limit and unfortunately we will have to bring our seminar to an end very soon. The tradesmen will be coming in shortly to install the new audio-visual equipment'.

'Ah, yes, I understand, of course, the equipage of the future'. Daladier drank from his glass and held the audience with his gaze. There had been movement, people picking up bags, getting ready to hurry from the room, some no doubt needing to find the toilets, but everything stilled as he began to speak once more.

'Yes, and so I will bring myself to the conclusion of my talk today. In my recent experiments I have struggled to explore the limits of the Book. I have learnt that its materiality, structure, imperative, voice, even its typography, constitute no more than a mirage. The Book is in fact a textual displacement of the potentialities of thought itself, whether that be the thought of the famous philosopher or the thought of the lonely and neglected writer. And so now I announce the end of the Book'. He gestured grandly at the books in the box at the rear of the room.

'It may seem strange to announce the end of the book in a book, but so be it for the present as our species has not yet liberated itself from reading. Rest assured though that before the end of your lifetime it will do so, and very definitely. The science of structural linguistics which underpins the human sciences will shortly be overrun by apparently marginal issues not comprehended by the existing questions of writing. The results will be cataclysmic in literature, history, and philosophy. Dear friends, bid farewell to our beloved written word, for writing erases that which separates one thing from another and creates tentacles which mystify the true nature of things. What creates the illusion of oneness arises from the coexisting illusion of not-one-ness; which is not any kind of connection or indeed a thing at all. Things emerge only from what separates them, there can be no simple beginning or origin, and hence no simple aim or end or indeed anything simple at all. Language has neither inside nor outside but refers only to elements of other things which refer themselves on again to other things and so on ad infinitum.

I understand you students will be spending the whole of the coming year reading and writing. Some of you will go on as scholars, no doubt, and write your own books. As you do so you will be formulating the last instances of a thousand-year heritage trembling at the edge of the abyss. The human species is deconstructing its texts and exploring the meaninglessness of meaning. Thank you kindly for allowing me to address you'.

The audience seemed stunned. A few people began to clap, others joined in. The students stared at one another. What had just happened? Daladier put his hand out to Professor Newton and grasped it firmly. He did not shake his hand, rather he held it, bending forward and holding his gaze.

'Thank you my friend for permitting me to speak today. I now must hurry away, I have a plane to catch this afternoon and a car is waiting'.

He glided from the room. It took a moment or two before the reaction started. Simone grabbed her things from under her chair and slid along the back of the wall. She wanted to say goodbye to Oscar and Derry but couldn't bear to wait another minute to get out of the crowd. She found a small corridor which went upstairs, and then led down again at the far end to a small door which pushed open easily. Long shadows traced their way across the grassy fields.

She went along a rough pathway and soon found a road and a bus shelter in the middle of a stand of dense bushes. A bus would go to the station in twenty minutes. That would be fine.

She wanted to get away from this weird place, go back to the harbourside breezes, the deep coolness of the old weatherboard house, the smell of turpentine and beeswax and something cooking, soup or beans.

She sensed the truth in what Daladier had said even though she didn't like it. There was something wrong with all this obsessive reading and writing. It had eaten up her mother's life. It made apparently rational people do ridiculous things which in turn wrecked other peoples' lives. Did she really want to go on with it? Would it eat her up as well? But what else was there to do? She thought she had escaped when she came back to Sydney, but now here it was again, the same stuff in a different guise. She had to get a scholarship so she could get her Honours degree, to get away from Christine and out of her dead father's house but she'd still be doing the same thing her mother, Serge, Daladier and all the others had spent their lives doing.

At least this expedition had shown her one thing: she did not want to move out to the hot lacklustre suburbs. She would stay near the city, where she felt at home. Paris had been home once: inner Sydney was home now. She would find a way to make it hers, on her own terms, never mind all the reading and writing it would take to get there. So what if it was pointless? It was better than working in a factory, as Serge had once made Sylvie do, so she could share the consciousness of the real working class.

The bus arrived and took her to a nearby railway station. There was so little life out here. At least there had been life, lots of life, abundant life, exciting life, in Paris. Still, being in this dull place was a means to an end. She must focus on what she was doing. She just had to find a way to do it with more grace and less resistance. Daladier had done it. Nobody could have imagined, back in the 1960s, struggling against his Algerian origins, that he would finish up being an acclaimed academic now leading the way in a philosophical revolution, least of all one against the book.

It had been extraordinary, seeing him again in the flesh, although it was a shame there was no-one to share this experience with. Maybe she should write to him. Did he even know her mother was dead? Had they kept in touch? She was sorry now she hadn't picked up a copy of his book, with his signature. Meredith was right. She should start thinking like an academic. Daladier would make an excellent patron.

4

SMALL MATTERS

I was a small person. You know, below average, not the usual size. It wasn't easy. Some people called me names. I hardly dared to go into a pub or club, people would stare and someone would always make a snide remark and it would turn into a fight. Don't think for a minute I would step away from a fight, no, far from it. I'd put up my fists to any man and give him a good whack in the guts, give him a shock, usually make him spew. They don't expect it, those bullies, they think you'll just slink away and let them have their fun at your expense.

Most of the time I didn't stand out. My hair is fair and rather fine. My erstwhile beloved used to say my eyes were blue as the Norwegian ice. I do have small feet and hands. For some reason ladies don't like that. But I kept myself in top condition through capoeira, one of the more obscure martial arts although it's quite popular these days.

In spite of my difficulties, I was pretty happy. There was plenty of everything. But you know how it is, we humans tend to think things can always be better. Would in fact be better if only … if only … more money, more power, more influence and so on. But I just wanted more me. Deep down I hated being small. Being short. Less than a real man. I mean, OK, Napoleon was short too and at least I wasn't fat like Danny DeVito, but there is something about smallness which puts people off. Unless you are a jockey, of course, in which case it's an asset, but unfortunately I am allergic to horses.

So I made my living as an extra in movies and acted in advertisements. Although I'm ashamed to confess it, when I was skint I worked in a porn show where I did unspeakable things to attractive ladies. I could see the piggy faces of the punters beyond the spotlight. It was disgusting that they could afford to come into a place like this and leer at a respectable man like myself forced to wear a leopard-skin leotard and spangled codpiece.

You can see why I was ready to jump at the chance of a better life. I could hardly believe my luck. I met her on the set of a feature film about secret agents tasked with exposing a terrorist group undermining some imaginary state in the Middle East. The terrorists were part of an international conspiracy. I was one of the secret agents and I excelled in the role, showing off my fighting skills in scene after scene. I was really the star of the show. For the first half of the movie I was in one of those black robe thingies with a little grill in the face, so everyone thought I was a local girl and then they got a real surprise when I flung it off and leapt over the balcony to take on the terrorists in hand-to-hand combat.

She was one of the ladies of the harem waiting to be liberated. She wore gauzy veils and gold jewellery. She didn't have to do much in the movie, just sit on cushions stuffing her face with Turkish delight. In the climax scene I was the only one of the secret agents small enough to get into the harem to foil the terrorists. I climbed in through a hole in the roof and shot them all dead just as they were forcing the ladies out the door before setting off a remote-control nuclear device in the Sultan's palace. Of course the Sultan was incredibly grateful and gave me the reward of a night with whichever one I fancied, and you can guess who I chose. The fade-out scene had me resting my head in her bosom while she leaned over, took another bite and gently touched her lips to mine.

They cut the scene there, but she went on anyway and kissed me properly, her teeth slightly sticky and her breath all sugar and almonds. Later that night she took me into her dressing room and made a proposition I will never forget. She spoke with such a sweet Northern accent.

'Come back with me to the city' she said. 'You'll never regret it'. She said I could live in her luxurious apartment overlooking the ocean, and what was more she knew someone who could 'fix me up'.

I didn't like that part. What about me needed fixing up? I went cold and distant, but she explained that it would be difficult for her to be seen around town and go to cocktail parties with such a small fellow especially as she had to wear very high heels to be taken seriously as an actress. I was angry but intrigued as well. What could be done about my size? I'd been told all my life it was a cross I had to bear, and I thought I'd born it with dignity, considering. But if there really was some way? Wouldn't it be worth trying?

So began my life in chains. She took me to a clinic somewhere out of the city and introduced me to a doctor, a smooth sleek silver fox. He beamed genially upon me and said I must have faith in him. He said I would have to undergo deep sleep therapy for a time while he worked his little hormonal miracles, and that after that I would need a maintenance dose every day. What he didn't say was that it was incredibly expensive, that she was paying for it, and she would be the one to dole out the doses.

Sure enough, I agreed. I was admitted to the clinic and I went to sleep. I have no idea how long I stayed asleep. The whole time was a blur. I remember waking up now and then, tubes going in and out, a hazy sense of space and time, then I was awake properly, and I ached and pained all over. But it was true, I'd grown, my legs stretched out before me, even my feet seemed bigger than before, my chest and waist were further away and it felt very strange.

Another couple of weeks passed while I got used to it, and she came to see me with bottles of French champagne and little trifles to amuse me. I didn't think what it meant, just that I was weirdly grateful. When it was time to leave she gave me a new hand-tailored Italian suit to wear, and I was as pleased as anything.

I didn't stop to ask myself why she was doing this. A beautiful, talented woman like her could have had any of a thousand men. In my ignorant pride I assumed it was because of my undoubted charm and special personality, not to mention my sexual prowess which she praised to the skies every day until I was so swollen with self-adoration I could hardly stop thinking about how wonderful I was.

I loved living in her luxurious apartment, I loved escorting her to elegant dinners and although she was still taller than me in her high heels it seemed socially acceptable. I suppose people thought I must be very rich, since the most beautiful women in the world often take up with short rich men. Maria Callas and Jacky Kennedy both fell for Aristotle Onassis.

She always introduced me as an actor, which was true enough, and I had a wonderful time sipping it with the glitterati, boogying at nightclubs and watching the dawn break over the ocean with a refreshing glass of Roederer.

Too good to be true? You know what they say. It took a year before things started to change. It wasn't her that changed, no, she remained the same. It was me. It was how I viewed the situation. Instead of enjoying myself trailing around after her to various functions I began to get annoyed that we always seemed to be doing what she wanted. If I refused to go somewhere, preferring to stay at home watching some old black and white movie, there was trouble. She'd storm about the apartment in her pink slip, haughty and cold, her nose in the air, making cutting remarks.

It was amazing how much drama she could insert into everything, like if I didn't feel like doing it one morning because I had a hangover or just wanted to read a book in peace there'd be all hell to pay, tears, screams, threats, the lot, but the greatest threat of all was my daily dose. She kept that mysterious medicine hidden away and made sure to remind me that if I missed a day I'd start shrinking again. On the rare occasions when she went out and left me alone in the apartment I'd look in every conceivable hiding place. I concluded that she must be carrying it around in her capacious handbag. It was her ultimate power and she never let herself get so drunk or stoned or whatever that she'd let me find it.

As time went on I became more and more irritated. She expected me to be at her side all the time, to pour her drinks and find her lipstick. If I sat down and waited for her to get me a drink I could have died of thirst. I existed to serve her needs, but as far as she was concerned I didn't have any, except to serve her.

I ask you, how could any self-respecting man put up with it? I needed to be treated with a certain level of respect. I knew that men scuttled off to have secret affairs with secretaries and air hostesses and that their women had to take it if they wanted to keep the credit cards. But if the women so much as looked at another man or chatted one up at a party they'd be in trouble for a week, or worse.

Men were meant to have the money and pay the bills, men made the travel arrangements and bought the cars, men basically were top dog. Oh sure, they'd let women think they had the upper hand, listen to their little complaints, humour them, let them get away with a bit of naughtiness, but it was all just to keep the wool over their eyes. The women would go out for little lunches with their girlfriends and bitch on about their men's affairs and meanness and halitosis and snoring and all the rest but at the end of the proverbial day everyone knew who was really in charge.

What was I to make of my situation? It couldn't go on like this, letting her get away with it. I started asserting myself, refusing to fit in with her plans, going out on my own, getting drunk at a bar with some fellows, and I enjoyed it, believe me I did, being one of the boys, and there we were ogling girls and telling rude jokes and laughing our heads off behind wifey's back.

I learnt how clever some of the boys could be, tricks that had never occurred to me, they knew how to say things that women liked, holding their hands and telling them there's nothing more important than a good relationship and how much they valued honest communication while thinking about some pretty waitress or the teacher at their son's kindie. When they were by themselves at the bar, they'd laugh at how the women would swallow it down, how easy it was to fool them. I couldn't stop thinking about all this stuff and soon I couldn't stand it every day when I had to be nice to her to get my lousy little dose of medicine.

It was while I was seething with frustration – a frustration I had to rigidly control so that she would never guess – that I began to suspect why she had chosen me in the first place. It wasn't my charm or sexual passion, it was because she could see how biddable I was. Where once I'd seen her as beautiful, warm and generous, I now saw she was a scheming evil bitch who'd taken a poor defenceless creature and reduced him to slavery so he had become a pathetic imitation of a man.

How could I forgive her? Should I even try? I had to bring into play all my acting skills which as I have indicated were quite considerable. I'd take her into my arms and murmur gently in her ear about how lovely she was, how warm and kind, while all the time I was staring at her reflection in the mirror opposite and looking at the wrinkles in her neck. I took careful note of all her minor imperfections, the pimples when her monthly time came around, how she swelled up and lost her fine sleek silhouette and would make a few carefully chosen remarks to draw attention to every pound she put on, letting a little bit of fat dimple up under my strong fingers to emphasise the cellulite. It made her nervous, I could see, but she was so sure of her power that it never caused her to consider the evil of her ways. I knew she still regarded me as her creature to do with as she would, and I couldn't stand the humiliation of it all.

One morning I woke early and looked at her. She did look beautiful as she slept, warmly curled up beside me. And no matter how wicked she was, I still found her very desirable, although I managed to control it most of the time. Now an interesting new idea came into my head. I waited till she began to stir, and then started to make love to her with all my most passionate skill. She responded, of course, and after I'd brought her to her pleasure a couple of times, I lay beside her my arm casually draped over her belly.

'Dearest' I said to her, 'Let's get married'.

I don't know what I thought she'd say. I thought she might at least consider it. But I hadn't bargained on her response.

'You!' she said, 'Marry you? Why on earth would I marry you? I can't imagine what you think of me, even to suggest such a thing'. She went on and on with cruel and harsh words until I couldn't stand it another minute and got up and locked myself in the bathroom. When I came out she was gone.

You can imagine my state of mind that day. To be treated like this by a mere woman! All my new-found male pride was bristling with fury. Yet as the day wore on and she didn't return my anger was replaced by anxiety, and finally fear. What if she didn't come back at all? Suppose she'd bought an air-ticket to Rome or London or Paris where she had numerous pretentious friends and open invitations to castles and luxury flats? What if she left me shut here in this apartment without my daily dose? Would I start to shrink? Would it be hideously painful? Would I even survive?

As the soft evening darkened into night I was in the most terrible state. Finally I flung myself out of the apartment and determined to do what I'd intended so often before but had never dared. I had to find the doctor who had treated me. When she'd taken me to the clinic I had only the vaguest notion of Sydney geography. Where to start? I remembered only that the place had large trees all around it and the air was clear and fresh. I hailed a taxi. The driver was an affable fellow.

'Listen old man' I said, 'I'm in a real spot. I need to find a place, but I don't know where it is. It's a hospital, a private clinic. I'll hire you for whatever you want all night long if necessary if you can help me find this place'.

I told him all I knew about it, that it was a large white building set among trees. I remembered a blue neon sign outside which was another clue.

'Sure' he said, 'I'll do what I can'.

So we set off. In my confused state I'd thought it might be easy.

'Roughly which way was it?' he asked. 'North, South, East or West?'

I didn't have any idea.

'Well' he said, 'Let's look up the phone book'.

Yes, this was all those years ago before Google and

stuff.

We found a pub and went inside and asked for the Yellow Pages. I had a couple of stiff whiskies while we wrote down the names of every private clinic in Sydney. There were a lot of them.

'We'll start with the south' he said, and we headed off through the night traffic. We went through Sylvania and Sutherland and Picnic Point, then we stopped for a coffee, then went up the northern line from Chatswood to Roseville to Pymble to Turramurra. But none were right, no blue neon signs, plenty of trees but not in the right order. A few times he asked me if I wanted to keep going, but by then I was desperate, I could feel funny things happening in my wrists and ankles and I knew we had to go on.

We went towards the west after that, through Normanhurst and Pennant Hills and Carlingford then out along the north-western road. Somehow this began to feel a bit more familiar, and I thought we were on the right track. Dawn found us up a side road.

'There's just one place up here' he said. 'Then if that's no good we'll have to call it a night, I have to knock off. We can try again tomorrow night if you like'.

I agreed but feared that by then it would be too late and I would already have started shrinking.

At the end of a narrow laneway we found it. I knew it at once, the neon sign was still on and now I recognised the name: Breuer's Private Clinic. The relief flooding through me was incredible. I had found it, I would be free at last! I paid the driver and paid him over again, so awash was I with gratitude.

'Good luck' he said as he drove away.

Inside it was cool and dim. There were signs on the walls with odd statements under glass. I noticed one as I sat down in the waiting room.

'Freedom lies in the extinction of desire'.

I couldn't imagine what that was supposed to mean, or what it was doing in a medical clinic. After a while I got sick of staring at it and went to find someone. There were a few snuffling noises but no-one was in sight. I thought they must all still be asleep although most medical facilities insist on waking patients at five in the morning.

Finally I came back to where I started, as if I'd walked around a great big circle. The pains were now shooting up to my knees and shoulders. I banged on the counter and shouted.

Finally a nurse appeared, a pretty woman with a kind face.

'Yes, can I help you sir?'

'Yes, yes, you must help me. I came here ... some time ago .... I must see the doctor, the doctor who treated me'.

'And who was that?' she asked gently.

'I don't know his name. Nobody told me. I don't think. But I must find him, it's very urgent.'.

She asked my name and lifted out an enormous ledger. Then she went to a filing cabinet and extracted a file.

'Ah yes, of course, you saw our Director Dr Breuer. You are lucky, he has been staying in his overnight apartment, perhaps he could see you now'.

She disappeared through a frosted glass door. I waited. My heart was beating and I could feel my pulse pushing against the side of my neck in a most uncomfortable manner. It was the drugs wearing off, I didn't know how long I could stand it.

Finally she returned. 'Follow me' she said. I followed her up and down twisting corridors until I was completely confused. We emerge into bright morning sunshine for a moment and crossed a courtyard into a low white building. On the veranda was a man drinking coffee. He looked up and smiled. It was him, no doubt about it.

'Do sit down'.

His voice was quiet and gentle.

'What can I do for you?'

'You know who I am?'

'Yes, I remember your case. Are you having difficulties?'

Difficulties! Well, I told him all about it then, it all came pouring out. I found myself pleading.

'So please, can you help me, give me the medicine so I can lead my own life, be free of her!'

I thought as one man to another he'd be sympathetic. Well, he was sympathetic, but what he said made me weak with shock.

'I'm sorry' he said, 'but we do live in a private enterprise system. You see, she has paid for your treatment and your drugs, and unless you can pay as much as she does, I can't do anything for you. Besides which she too is a patient, and I prescribed the cure for her'.

'Her?' I gasped. 'There's nothing the matter with her!'

'Well, not in the way that there's something the matter with you. But she too has a problem. Her problem is that she needs to control a man. Hence, I told her she needed to find a man she thought she could control. And she found you. I told her what I could do for you, but I'm doing it for her as well'.

'But that's unethical' I protested. 'Isn't it?'

'To help two people at once?' he asked, sipping his coffee. 'Hardly. And in any case the purpose, for there is a purpose, is that you both will learn that satisfying what you think is your desire will not really satisfy you. She has what she wants yet she is not happy because she knows that you want to escape and so she must contrive to hold you more and more tightly, yet as she does so she realises that it is her will and not yours, which is not what she wants, for she wants a willing slave, not an unwilling one. And you are not happy, because you are now a normal man, but you cannot be a normal man while she controls you'.

He smiled, revealing large super-white teeth.

'But the pains in my legs and arms! You're a doctor, you must help me'.

'Indeed' he said, 'but I cannot help you in the way you want unless you have somehow come into a rather large fortune. You have a choice. You can return to her, and accept the life you have created together, or you can return to your former self. I can give you treatment to prevent pain while it is happening but I cannot stop it happening'.

'But this is monstrous, gross, immoral! Can't you reconsider? I beg you, I implore you!'

I was reduced almost to tears at what had been done to my life – my precious life, the only one I would ever have. How could she and this horrible doctor have conspired to ruin it so?

He gazed at me and sipped his coffee.

'Well, since you have come here, and found me, and since I assume you don't have enough money to exceed her contract, there could be another way. I would require you to put yourself into my hands, rather than hers. I can release you from her contract, but you'll have to give yourself to me'.

'Why? What would you want from me?'

I was horrified at the thought of exchanging a mistress for a master. On the other hand, perhaps with a man it would not be so bad.

He looked at me speculatively.

'I am not sure yet' he said. 'But your case interests me greatly. Most unusual. And you yourself are an unusual person. I could learn from you'.

'What do you mean, use me in experiments?'

'Perhaps' he replied, 'but it would be nothing painful, not more painful than what you have already experienced and are experiencing now'.

And indeed, he was right. The pains were pressing up into my chest and neck and my breathing was becoming constricted. It was terrifying. I hated him sitting there in the early morning sun with his coffee, but what choice did I have? I could return to her on my bended knees and beg her forgiveness and give up forever any hope of freedom or I could take my chances with Dr Breuer and who knows? Perhaps find an even better existence. This is the kind of thing that happens to people like me all the time.

Well. So I agreed.

He put me to sleep again. It was just like the time before, only this time I didn't feel so disoriented, in fact it was altogether quite comfortable drifting in and out of consciousness, not worrying how long it was taking or anything like that.

When I finally woke up it was a nice blue morning

with sun coming in behind the blinds. There was birdsong outside and as I looked around the room, I saw huge bunches of flowers everywhere. For a mad moment I wondered if she had taken pity on me and brought me back. I stretched, and felt my legs and arms move. It felt good. I looked down and saw my feet. They seemed somehow more dainty, slender.

I decided to get out of bed even though sitting up made me feel dizzy. I put my feet down on the ground. Something in my legs seemed not quite right, the muscles didn't seem the same. Probably from being in bed for so long. I looked at my hands and arms, they seemed slimmer too. Perhaps he'd really stretched me out. It was only when I was standing up that I knew something odd had happened. My chest felt funny. I looked down at the white hospital coat. That was when I first suspected.

I sat down on the bed again. He couldn't have! It wasn't possible. I had to know. I fumbled with the ties on the gown and pulled it off. What can I say? How can I describe the awful feeling, the horror as it came true before my eyes, and I saw the pink swellings between my arms and, horror of horrors, what was below my belly, or rather what wasn't. I lay back on the bed, pulled the covers over me, and felt tears seeping down into the pillow.

He came in then.

'Ah' he said. 'I see you've woken up! Haven't I done a lovely job? Do you want to look?'

I gazed at him mutely.

'Come now darling, you'll get used to it soon enough. Do you like the lovely flowers I got for you? See the roses? That gorgeous dusty pink. It's a new variety called

Evening Passion. And here's some beautiful scent, L'Aphrodite, French of course, only the best for my darling.' He came over and sprayed this cloying smell on me till I reeked like the Sultan's harem, where all this nightmare had started.

'Can I … Ca …?' My voice? It had gone high and breathy. 'Can I … go back?'

'Back! Back! Never. Now I've really created you, a beautiful new full-size human…'

'Go on, say it' I flounced. 'Woman!'

'And nothing wrong with that. Here's to the fair sex'. He popped open a bottle of champagne he had hidden in his white coat. I wanted to puke all over his horrible roses.

So you see this is how it is with me. If it's not a faux prince or a circus-master, it's some selfish woman or a weird rich doctor. It's not so bad being his wife, except when I remember back to what it was like being a man. I try to keep away from football and things which remind me. And yes, I've seen her again. She came into the clinic, still so beautiful but very sad. I was pleased thinking how sorry she must be that she'd treated me like that, especially over the marriage business.

But then the strangest thing happened. My new husband of course was still her doctor. And it occurred to me that his continuing attention to her might be more than purely professional. So now I have to keep a very close eye on him, and if I see her anywhere around the place I kick up the devil of a fuss. If I find out that he's carrying on behind my back he'll be sorry, very sorry indeed, and believe it or not, I really know how to make him suffer now, which at least is some compensation.

5

CHRISTMAS KISS

Rosa didn't expect to see Leonard. She was here to collect Eddie, her son, her sweet tow-headed baby now a handsome and haughty young man. She wasn't sure she liked this new version much. She was driving him to horrible Heathrow. For many years the two of them had Christmas lunch together in a swank hotel dining room, Claridges' or the Dorchester. He always paid with one of several highly reflective credit cards. This year he cancelled their little lunch.

He was going to Sydney to stay with fiancée Pandora, apparently descended from some minor aristocrats who had relocated to the sunny Antipodes. She had just finished a Masters in Art History at the Slade and Eddie was totally smitten. Pandora was equally thrilled to have Eddie's dad Leonard as a father-in-law. She'd left for Sydney already but Eddie couldn't get away from work. He would be spending Christmas day on the plane. But he wouldn't suffer - there would be plenty of champagne and fine food in Business Class. He had spent Christmas Eve in the once-again-renovated Islington house now worth millions, with his father and stepfather. Rosa supposed that was the right term for one's father's male partner. Or maybe it should have been father and father? Or fathers?

After driving Eddie to the airport she would return to her empty flat and drink something alcoholic, but not too much of it, and that would be her Christmas Day. It didn't matter. She didn't want to do anything on Christmas Day. As if she believed in Christmas. How was it possible whole countries full of atheists lavished so much time and money on a festival none of them believed in?

Once she celebrated the winter solstice with the women's collective. Pagans, Druids and witches still celebrated at Stonehenge. Were Druids feminists? Boudicca for instance? Many said so. It didn't make much sense from the viewpoint of history, but you couldn't let the side down. She was glad she had left all that behind. Collective living was just too hard. On the other hand she had to admit she was increasingly lonely. She was just another retired academic with no friends living in a vaguely quaint flat in Kentish Town. She felt displaced by time. It was too weird, knowing it was nearly the end of the millennium.

The traffic was light, the air very cold with a little snow. She shouldn't be driving Eddie to Heathrow. He could just as well take the train, or a taxi, as he pointed out several times. She found herself surprisingly determined. She wanted to see him off at the airport. She felt, she knew, that this was a momentous transition: Eddie was leaving her, flying to the far side of the planet, to the place she had fled when she was young, her 'home' but that was so long ago and she couldn't imagine what it would be like, to go back. There was nothing for her there now.

She loved Eddie so much. She had never loved anyone else the way she loved him, not Leonard, not her girlfriends when she had any, definitely not her own mother. Being a mother was a bitter beverage her mother used to say, and it turned out she was right. The pain of losing him, trying to pretend it was fine, hoping he would come back to her, longing to hear his voice, wanting to feel his arms around her, to be reassured of his love: it never let up. She always thought he would stay near her as she aged, to the bitter end, whatever that might be. And now he was talking about going to live in bloody Australia.

Who was Eddie really? Doesn't a mother know her own son? Increasingly she thought, probably not. Love for your children blinded you. All along there had been a secretive side to Eddie, intensifying as he became an attractive young man convinced of his own rightness. She thought sometimes he was just acting like a son, with the birthday cards and flowers, "Love always, Eddie". She realised that she didn't interest him. He didn't care about what she thought or her ideas or the papers she had written, the talks she had given, the reading groups, the important academics who had once praised her. She sometimes thought he felt pity, even contempt. But she couldn't let go, the maternal matrix never stopped its seduction, its breathy whispering that kept her thinking he was a devoted boy who would always love his mother.

Ever since he moved into his smart new flat in Camden Town they had been drifting apart and in the past year he could hardly be bothered to talk to her. The writing had long been on the wall and instead of fading it was getting darker. He was still a teenager when he declared that he did not want to live with her and the 'gang of witches' as he once called them, even though he did apologise later. He wanted to live with his father and his father's partner Alexei. The loss of his everyday presence in her life made tears spring to her eyes and her heart wince.

She had to face it, he preferred them to her. Later, with his remarkable income as a merchant banker he found his own place and Pandora moved in. He had been living with her for six months before he thought to mention it to Rosa. He did not ask her over. When she insisted she wanted to meet the girl, they invited her to tea at Claridges'.

She smoothed down her sensible skirt at a red light.

The traffic moved along and she paid attention to the road, to the cars, to the other drivers. She could always focus on the things that were right in front of her, push aside troubling thoughts, maintain a cheerful smile, be at her best. She had done it forever. It was a matter of getting through things and going on with a semblance of order and a sense of humour.

The line of cars thickened. She checked her watch, anxious, taking deep breaths. Her heart was beating too fast, as it did whenever she thought she would be late. She hadn't mentioned it to the doctor. She didn't believe in Western medicine anyway or so she told herself when she felt well.

Approaching Islington she began to worry about where she would park. Eddie would have a large suitcase, he always packed so many clothes. She came into the street and scanned the row. Of course the road was full of Christmas visitors. She took out her phone to call him: she might have to double park and wait.

But just as she slowed a car pulled out. It left more space than she needed for her modest Volvo. In the mirror she looked at her face. The pale light did not flatter her: she looked worn, she had wrinkles beside her eyes and mouth, much older than last year.

She had rubbed light makeup over the dark spots on her cheeks, and dabbed some on her hands, a legacy of hot summers, which she bitterly regretted now. It had been lovely to lie about baking on beaches in Ibiza or on the Cote d'Azur. Who knew? Back when Leonard had loved her, or at least seemed to love her, a young mother-goddess with long blonde hair and large breasts, lying in the sun half naked seemed perfect. When had he decided she wasn't what he wanted? How did that happen? She had never asked him, couldn't. They had become so painfully polite and hardly spoke except when it was about Eddie.

Parked now in front of the house, she looked up at the grand frontage. She switched off the engine, opened the car door, and stepped into the frigid air. At the top of the stairs she paused, thinking better of it. She turned to go back to the car, but the door swung open suddenly. Eddie's face and thatch of fair hair appeared.

'Oh, you're here' he said. 'Merry Christmas'.

'Yes of course darling, Merry Christmas'.

She wanted to kiss him, but he was too far away. And he wouldn't have liked it.

'Well,' she said. 'Are you ready?'

'Sorry, not quite. Come in for a minute'.

'Oh, I don't want to disturb anyone'.

'Alexei and the others have gone over to his aunt's Russian Christmas lunch party. Dad's still here. He's watching the dinner'.

A vacuum cleaner buzzed somewhere. The cold air rushed in behind her. Eddie pushed the door shut.

His suitcase was still open at the bottom of the stairs.

'I forgot to put in my swimming things' he said, pressing a large plastic bag onto the top of the bulging contents. 'Hard to believe it will actually be hot in Sydney'.

'You shouldn't force it' she said. He glanced up at her with that annoying mixture of superiority and irritation.

The vacuum cleaner stopped, and Leonard appeared in the hallway. He was wearing a pinafore. They both stood very still.

'Hullo there' he said. 'Merry Christmas'.

She was astonished. She still imagined him smooth, golden skinned, well groomed. Even as he got older and his hair went grey, he had always looked somehow perfect for whatever situation they were in. Last time she had seen him was at Eddie's graduation. Eddie insisted on a set of family photographs: himself, her, Leonard, Alexei. The family.

He had been achingly polite, kind, courteous, asking about her job, her new flat. He and Eddie laughed and joked together. Leonard's new book, on the art of Abram Arkhipov, had just been published to great acclaim. He was pleased with himself. It was she who had pointed out to him the depictions of the life of Russian women in Arkhipov's work and described it as displaying a revolutionary incipient feminism. The reviewers loved that phrase.

'Hullo' she said, and smiled, an uneasy half-smile. The vacuum cleaner was still dragging along behind him.

'Housework?' she asked and realised at once how silly that sounded.

Through the double doorway she saw an elegant room, filled with Christmas decorations and a dramatic tree whose lights switched on and off in a complex pattern. Opened presents lay around the room, cast aside, as if they were not good enough.

'Cleaning up' he said. 'The nephews are a bit of a handful. Thought I'd pitch in while they were gone'.

'Nephews?'

'Alexei's sister's boys. You've met them? No? Oh well, bad luck. They're cute kids'. He smiled, showing dimples alongside over-white teeth. Once she thought he was cute too.

How old he looked now. His face was puffy, he had large bags under his eyes, his hair was receding, he had strange marks on his face, swellings, as though he had been bitten by mosquitoes. But there were no mosquitoes in London in winter.

They both stepped forward. She did not know whether she should try to kiss him. Would he offer to kiss her? They stood, unable to move. As she looked at his ageing, tired face she was flooded with memory. Their days as squatters in London. They couldn't resist each other, that's how it seemed. He became her lover right away and she accepted it without a murmur, moving in with him the same week. The two of them, arm in arm in the sunshine. The quiet, private wedding. Him helping her into the hospital bed as she groaned and stuttered, gripped by labour pains. His smile as he looked at the neatly wrapped baby parcel and kissed her cheek tenderly, telling her that he loved her.

They were both so young. They lived on one floor of the vast decaying squat. After Eddie came along, they were even more deliriously happy. Then Alexei turned up and that was that.

Could this slightly dishevelled puffy person be the same man who had caused so much heartache for all those years? Could she kiss that wrinkly face with the ugly mottled marks? She didn't think so. She turned to Eddie.

'Are you ready now?' she asked.

Eddie lifted his bag onto its wheels. Leonard put his arms around Eddie, gave him a warm hug. Eddie hugged him back.

'Take care over there,' said Leonard. 'And give my regards to Pandora'.

'Bye Dad. And Happy Christmas'.

'Yes, for sure'. He was grinning as Eddie wheeled his suitcase to the door. She followed awkwardly.

'So long' he said. Eddie opened and closed the door and lugged the suitcase down the front steps and across to her car. He pulled at the boot impatiently.

'Honestly mother, I don't know why you are doing this. I could cope perfectly well on my own'.

She realised he was embarrassed and hurt. She and Leonard, they should have kissed, a kiss which would have recognised the past, all that had been between them, the good and the bad, everything that had produced this young man who was at that moment frowning in irritation as he pulled his scarf around his neck, waiting for her to press the remote.

'Come on' he said, 'It's freezing out here'.

Numbly she heard the doors unlock. He heaved his case into the back. She went to the driver's side and climbed in, starting the engine in silence. As she pulled away from the curb she looked into the rear-view mirror and saw the outline of a face peering from the window, fading quickly as she drove away.

Eddie gazed ahead, not looking at her. There was pain in him, and anger. Now he would go to Australia and after that anything could happen.

At the airport she hugged him to her as long as she could. 'I love you Eddie', she whispered. Perhaps he did not hear. He patted her on the back, as one does with a difficult elderly relative.

'Merry Christmas mother' he said, looking over her shoulder then swept away into the chaos of Heathrow. It was far too late to kiss anyone. She drove home, her lips tingling.

6

─────

TOO RICH FOR ME

I met Amanda in the local pub. It was hot that night. The sea-breeze hadn't turned up. I was into my third light ale, but Bert my neighbour was well away. He's my neighbour on the farm, and my neighbour in the bar, if you see what I mean. I've been next to Bert, one way or another, for years now. We're old bachelors. Well, not so old, but into our fifties. Bert was looking grizzled. He didn't shave often and his ponytail was grey. He always wore a T-shirt. He did get dressed up for young Cathy's wedding, but even then he still wore a T-shirt. Most of his T-shirts came from 70s rock concerts, AC/DC, Cold Chisel, INXS, Midnight Oil, you know the line-up.

It seems damned unfair that Bert can drink as much as he likes but I'm on this low-alcohol caper. The doctor says I have to do it. The ticker started playing up, so I had one of those stent things put inside, it hurt like the devil even though the doc said that it didn't. Settled down now, but still doesn't feel quite right. Anyway, he said I had to lose weight, exercise, all the usual palaver, and especially I had to knock off the grog.

I wouldn't say I was a heavy drinker. Never was, even in my younger years. But the bottle's always been a pal of mine. When things go wrong, he's always there, reliable. I like a few beers and the odd OP rum. Mum and Dad drank OP rum until the day they died. It did them no bloody harm, they both lived into their 80s. How they'd laugh at the way things are these days.

I took over the farm. Dad always expected it, and I couldn't let him down. I was the fourth generation. The first Henderson was a cedar-getter, you can still see a few enormous stumps up in the back hills, they knew what hard work was in those days, then there was a bit of gold and then the old feller cleared the hillsides and it was all bananas. Dad never thought I would do anything else, it was up to me to carry on the family name. But somehow I never could find a suitable female to breed with, the local girls all wanted to work in town or move to Sydney.

Then young Cathy went to live in Western Australia, she's got four kids now and I hardly ever hear from her. She must be pretty busy. To tell the truth I thought we'd probably stay on the farm, run it together, brother and sister, a lot of families do that around here. But young Cathy really wanted to get married. I couldn't believe it when she said she'd met someone. On the Internet, she said. I don't approve of this Internet business. People should marry people they know, from their own district, that way they've got some idea what they're getting into. But this cove turned out to be one of those Serbians or Bosnians or whatever. He'd been opal-mining in Cooper Pedy. I didn't think much of him at first, but Cathy married him. Cosmic's his name, something like that, and it seems to have turned out all right. She had two kids one after the other and then the twins. Good on her. Her clock had been ticking for quite a while.

With Cathy gone I started feeling pretty lonely, and it had got worse recently. I found I was thinking about marriage. I tried to talk it over with Bert, but he clammed up. He's my best mate and I know he'd do anything for me, but everyone draws the line somewhere, and that's his line, the private stuff.

So it was very hot, and we were drinking in the front bar when these two birds walked in and made themselves at home. One was tall with blonde curly hair; the other was plump and dark. It was hard to say how old they were. The blonde came over and ordered gin and tonic. I still haven't got used to women in the public bar. It used to be simple, ladies belonged in the lounge. These ones didn't look rough or anything, but they were a bit too easy going to be ladies. They downed a couple of drinks and laughed a lot. A few fellers were taking looks at them. Spare women are hard to come by in these parts.

I watched them drinking gin and tonic and talking. They didn't talk too loudly but they were pretty lively, chatting away with each other. The blonde came over to order again. Up close you could see a lot of lines around her face, but she had nice white teeth and pretty grey eyes. There was something warm about her, creamy. She leaned on the bar next to me.

'Hullo' she said. I looked around, but it was me she was talking to.

'Hullo'. I didn't know what else to say.

'I'm Amanda' she said.

'Jack Henderson' I said and shook her hand. I'm not sure if you are meant to shake hands with women in the bar, but I did it anyway. She smiled.

'Pleased to meet you Jack.' She picked up the drinks and walked back to their table near the open window. Then she went over and put on a song on the juke box. Not many places still have juke boxes, it's one of the things I like here. I like that singer, too. What's her name, Bonny Rait?

'You reckon she could be your baby tonight?' Bert muttered, downing his drink.

'What do you mean?'

'Maybe looking for fellers'. He winked at me. They had makeup on, lipstick and such, their hair was soft and kind of boofy, and the blonde, Amanda, had the top couple of buttons of her shirt open. They were dressed to attract all right but there was this thing about their age, it made me uncomfortable. With all those creams and nips and tucks these days you just don't know any more.

Bert wanted to keep drinking but I was sick of light beer. I could see the girls had finished their drinks already, so I walked over to their table and said 'Can I get you another?'

They looked at each other. 'Why not?' said Amanda. 'Come over and join us'.

Well I couldn't help it, I was that pleased with myself. I got a gin and tonic too and carried all three over on a little tray. Bert glared at me.

'You want to come over?' I asked him. I was hoping he'd say no. He looked rough, and sometimes, after too many, he talked rough as well.

But you couldn't have held him back with a dog chain.

He was straightening his pants and tucking his T-shirt in right away. We sat down with these two – Amanda's friend was called Sherry, it suited her perfectly – and soon we were chatting away like nobody's business. Amanda told us that she was moving into town, she'd bought the old butcher's shop on the main street and was going to turn it into a craft shop, maybe sell afternoon teas out the back.

'A lot of work involved' observed Bert, who had a good eye for property and buildings and so on from his years as a carpenter.

'Yes', said Amanda, 'I know. But money's no object'.

That's not something you hear often. Even if money is no object, people don't like to say so. But Amanda was quite open about it. It was one of those stories. Her dad came from up this way. She had always liked it here, the sugar cane and the bananas, the blue calm sea, the breezes. But he had a proper profession, some kind of money thing, in Sydney, so they only came on holidays to see the grandies. After one thing or another, her dad died and left everything to her. She said she was 'quite comfortable'.

Sherry had plenty to say as well. Living as I do, alone, with hardly any company, I found it hard to keep all the information together. I got things mixed up, whose mother remarried, who lived where when. Amanda seemed so open, honest, but when I got to thinking about it later – next morning, in fact, head a shocker thanks to the gin – I couldn't quite work it out. It seemed unbeliev-able that a pretty woman would turn up in our town to open a business – a business for which there would be practically no demand, although I didn't want to burst her bubble by telling her that. But it was true. There were hardly any tourists here, and who else would want to buy bits of 'craft', pots and lace and all that, or have 'afternoon tea' in some tatty back yard? But then, if she was well off, she wouldn't need the business to make money in the first place.

I'm always a bit suspicious. If something looks too good to be true, then there you go. They were staying at Nan O'Grady's Luxury Guest House, and we walked them home. On the way, Amanda took my arm, like we were old friends.

'See you tomorrow night?' she said.

'Yeah, sure' I said, but by the time we got back to the ute I was pretty sure there was something funny going on. I said as much to Bert. He just laughed in my face.

'You're a stupid bastard sometimes. You can't tell when the butter's on the right side of the bread'.

'So you think they're OK?'

'Sure' he said, 'Nice girls'.

We saw the girls over the next few evenings. On Saturday night Bert invited us all up to his place for dinner. I'd never been invited to dinner at his place, last time I was there it was full of old newspapers and mouse-droppings. But he had everything cleaned up and ship-shape and cooked some excellent steaks on the old barbecue out the back. He'd made fresh salad, and boiled some potatoes with mayonnaise no less, and there was a fruit cake for dessert. He reckoned he'd made it himself. I didn't know whether to believe him but you don't say something like that. It was good cake too.

I'd be lying if I said I wasn't getting keen. Amanda seemed to like me. She leaned forward when she talked and had a sweet breath. She didn't smoke, just as well because I hate to see women smoking. Sometimes she touched my arm or put her hand on mine. I was feeling things I hadn't felt for years. Maybe ever.

Then a week or two later I asked her out, just the two of us. I drove twenty k to the next town, where there was a fancy restaurant near the sea. We had a great night. She drank white wine, but I stuck to the light stuff and then water. I left quite a big tip, which is not like me. When we were leaving, she dropped her handbag. You know what women's handbags are like, always stuffed full, so when everything falls out it goes everywhere, lipsticks and notebooks and aspirin and the rest. But she had it back in place in no time and was already well out the door when the young waiter came running up with an envelope in his hand.

'You forgot this' he said.

'Thanks' I said, and put it in my back pocket without thinking.

I took Amanda back to Nan O'Grady's that night in a bit of a state. I was thinking over and over: could I or couldn't I? When we said goodnight she kissed me. It wasn't a very long kiss, more a quick peck, but I caught that fresh creamy scent of her flesh and I thought, why not? There was nothing to stop me. The worst thing that would happen was she would say no. On the other hand, it still worried me that I didn't know how old she was.

I couldn't sleep and poured myself a cold beer. The envelope lay on the kitchen table, I'd taken it out of my pocket when I came in. It was already open, I didn't think whether it was mine or Amanda's, or so I told myself. Liar. I was curious.

It was a bank statement. I looked on the second page,

at the balance. When I saw it, I thought I would fall over. I mean, I wouldn't class it as an absolute fortune, but it was more than I ever imagined any one person could have in the bank, let alone a single woman.

It's strange, but just one glimpse of those black figures at the bottom of a sheet of paper changed everything. Next morning I burnt the envelope and its contents in the bin out the back. I didn't go to town that night, or the next. I didn't want to talk about it to anyone. I did my shopping early and went home and read the newspapers. I knew it was over with Amanda. It was that simple: she wasn't just a bit old, she was too rich for me. A man has to have some pride. I stayed away from town for weeks.

Finally I went back to the bar. I was missing Bert. I asked the barman if he'd been in. 'No, haven't seen him for a bit. Said he was going off somewhere'.

It wasn't like Bert not to tell me where he was going.

A while later an envelope came in the mail. I left it on the table under a newspaper. In the end I had to take a look. It was a wedding invitation. Amanda and Bert. My head was spinning, it was that much of a shock. I thought of Bert, togged up in a tuxedo, marrying rich creamy old Amanda. Later on he phoned. Asked me to be his best man. After all he was my mate. What could I say?

I made a real effort, the penguin suit and all. There were photos of the wedding in the local paper. They took over the whole pub and people turned up from everywhere, Amanda's old friends, Sherry and her mates, locals, everyone Bert had ever met. It was a good bash, I'll say that.

I know it could have been me. But there are some men who take things as they come, and some who don't. I guess I'm wedded to the past. They're living in the old butcher shop now, Bert and Amanda. He's done the whole place over and it looks great. They fixed up the back garden and the place is full of tourists sitting under fake palm trees eating scones with jam and cream and buying junk.

We still have a drink in the pub from time to time, but it's never been the same. Maybe he didn't even know how much she had. I wouldn't have either if I hadn't been such a snoop. Serves me right I guess. But what if I'd found out after we were married? Still, people these days don't seem to worry much about this kind of thing: women being richer than their husbands, or older. Sherry's coming up for a holiday soon. I wonder how she'd feel about it, living up here?

7

———

VODKA AND REINDEER

I met my first husband in 1962. You may have heard of Dr Magnus Binswinger. He was a Distinguished Professor at Humboldt University in East Berlin. He specialised in the analysis of Primitive Communist societies and the obstacles to their transition. He was born near Heidelberg and studied there as a young man. He thought he would be a philosopher. But politics intervened, and he became a codebreaker.

I have to tell you, he was a very good codebreaker. Anything I said he would go to work on right away. If I complained that his dietary requirements were too difficult to meet, he said it was on account of my imaginative limitations. This was a major flaw in my character, and although it might not matter intellectually it was affecting his health. In those days I worked on the translation of manuscripts from the Ancient Near East which was another kind of code-breaking although he did not agree with me on this point either.

He claimed he had become a vegetarian. By this he meant he would not eat actual pieces of meat. What he wanted was plenty of meat-based broth with a variety of vegetables cut into complicated shapes.

At one time in Germany we enjoyed a modest affluence – not like our present abundance, but even so there was no end of meat. Slaughterhouses worked around the clock killing the fat white pigs which provided so much of our hearty diet, our *Berlinerwürsten* and *Eisbein*, and there were chickens and ducks, and plenty of fish both salt-water and fresh from the seas, lakes and streams. And the Gypsies brought many kinds of wild meat to town. Herr Professor Doktor, as he insisted I call him, was particularly fond of wild hare, which was a specialty of the region where he grew up. Wild hare makes a nutritious and tasty soup. With plenty of vegetables and dumplings it is a meal fit for a king. Indeed, I believe King Otto of Bavaria had been so fond of it that he had had some twenty peasants engaged in nothing but hunting hare for his table. It was rumoured that any chefs who tried to record the castle's secret recipes were executed.

I too had eaten my share of it, but that was before the war, and I was a mere child. Later it was another story. You know what happened towards the end of the war when there was almost nothing to eat at all. As a teenage girl I enjoyed a nice bowl of rat soup more than once, while the bombs rained down outside and the fires burnt all over the city.

Herr Professor Doktor had suffered. He was sent to the Russian front in 1943, which didn't improve his digestion or his temper. Although he was supposed to be a codebreaker, they declared him a doctor instead. Did I mention that he was among the youngest ever to gain his doctorate? Even though he told them he knew not the first thing about medicine, by the end there were no real doctors left so the academic doctors had to put down their books – I speak in jest of course because most of them had been burnt – and take up the scalpel, or at least learn to tie a bandage. It wasn't much comfort to the poor wretches whose hands and feet were falling off with frost-bite but maybe it was better than nothing.

The conditions were dreadful, day after day and night after night of freezing temperatures, if they had anything to eat it was half-rotted potatoes or sour bread. After the war meat of any kind was still difficult to obtain in East Germany, and since the Nazis had eliminated the Gypsies they didn't come around anymore with their cargo of fresh-caught game. The starving peasants and fleeing soldiers had eaten every remaining wild animal or bird. You'll notice still in Berlin there's hardly a living thing, apart from people and dogs. During the war they ate dogs as well. And I believe the giraffe in Zoo Garden was delicious.

Herr Professor Doktor was senior to me. He was born in 1917 to a rather old mother – well in today's terms she wasn't old, only about 38 or so, but in those days women married early, had children early and mostly died early, thoroughly worn out. His mother was of peasant stock and his father was a descendent of Prussian Junkers come down in the world. Fighting in the trenches near the end of the first war he took a bullet in the face as a result of which he was not identified for quite some time. His wife

Emilie was left with five older children and Magnus the baby.

Resourceful and determined, she went back to her natal village with little more than the clothes she stood up in and a few possessions wrapped in cloths tied to sticks, carried by each of the little children as they walked along wearing rags on their feet.

But in the rural areas it was quite peaceful, and my husband grew up well enough in his mother's warm and large family. His extraordinary mind shone with particular brilliance in this worthy but limited environment. He taught himself to read from the schoolbooks of his older brothers, and then educated himself in tolerably grammatical Latin from a couple of old books belonging to his grandfather, unearthed from a wooden chest.

The local schoolmaster quickly noticed the remarkable qualities of this serious boy. Perhaps it was the strange conditions of the time, as society crumbled and the thugs took over with their marching and shouting, but whereas a person of Magnus's social background could not possibly have progressed under previous conditions, now it was as if the world opened up before him. He was able to disappear into his books and his study. When war broke out, he was already half-way through his degree. They allocated him duties in the Central Communications Department and for a time he worked on his dissertation under the secret supervision of Karl Jaspers.

Karl Jaspers had been kicked out of his Chair of Philosophy in Heidelberg in 1937 but he and his wife remained at liberty and he managed to continue his thinking and writing in secret. He was of course deeply troubled about everything that had happened, not least the way in which his friend and fellow-philosopher Martin Heidegger had seemingly embraced the Nazis.

On the occasional secret visit to Berlin, he poured out his heart to Magnus, which was touching but didn't help with the thesis. Magnus proposed to reconstruct the anti-metaphysical basis of Being and Time, but this project no longer found favour with Jaspers and so he was obliged to change direction rather suddenly.

I hasten to say that Magnus had no time for the Master Race and the Übermensch and all that but he had to consider that small cows also make poop, as his mother would say. So, like many others, he went along with things, completing his thesis only weeks before being sent to the Russian front. It was entitled 'Existential Ontology and Authentic Anxiety in the Light of German Philosophy'. Not one copy of this weighty tome exists today. Five years of tortured analysis and writing disappeared from the face of the earth.

I know all this, and a lot more, from the letters Herr Professor wrote to me early in our marriage. In 1962 I was a spinster of 31 and he was 45. Events after the war were so peculiar. I was an adaptable young woman and finding myself a Communist living in the German Democratic Republic was not such a surprise. But for Magnus – a rather unrealistic person at the best of times – to go from being a Heideggerian philosopher to a Nazi code-breaker to a military doctor in a filthy field hospital and then a dedicated Historical Materialist in the new DDR was quite difficult. These transitions deeply affected his personality.

I did my best. We met at a university function to welcome new students from Africa and I was very impressed. He was moderately tall with abundant dark hair which showed no signs of grey although he had been through so much. Our courtship was very brief. He told me he was looking to marry as his career prospects were being inhibited due to suspicions regarding his bachelorhood. His enemies were circulating rumours on account of his influence with the Rektor.

He was quite matter of fact. There was no business about love or desire. I was quite pretty, although rather short and dark for most men who in those days continued to crave the blonde from Valhalla. He said he liked me for my conversation. Looking back, I realise this was actually my ability to listen to him. It was worthwhile listening to him because he always had something interesting to say. We began well enough. After our marriage, attended only by a couple of colleagues, we settled immediately into a reconstructed flat on Warschauer Strasse. It was quite a smart address, such as smart addresses went in East Berlin in the 1960s, and I queued up to buy curtain material and tableware. He said he admired my homemaking abilities.

But after only one or two years it was apparent that the balance of admiration had changed. I was obliged to continue admiring him as much as I possibly could, whereas he didn't feel obliged to admire me very much, and soon not at all. On the contrary, I became the subject of an endless series of complaints. There are plenty of men like this, I now understand, who find the most peculiar satisfaction in diminishing the self-esteem of their wives.

But, although he tried to convince me I was mentally limited, he had no idea how strongly I would resist. Above all I was determined that his criticism would not affect me, or at least that I would not show any signs of it. No matter how cold and cruel, how harsh and unkind he was, I would accept it without comment and get on with things. His desire to affect me negatively was matched by my desire to remain unaffected, which made for a perfect balance in our relationship, even if at times it resembled a vast cold moonscape.

What I found most infuriating and most difficult to counter was his ceaseless critique of my cooking, a matter I have already mentioned but perhaps did not emphasise enough. It wasn't that he criticised the taste or the presentation, now it was the fundamental theoretical basis of the dish. His Marxist approach applied to everything. Cooking turned out to be one of the main problems of Transition. Wild meats represented the Primitive Communist level. Transition required us to leave that untroubled pre-domesticated hunting economy and move to a more scientifically advanced form of cuisine. The Communist Man of the future would live entirely on vegetable products, but for the moment it was necessary to meld the power of the rough foods of our original diet with the more advanced and highly evolved grains and vegetables.

So, for example, potatoes and rye were relics of the unreconstructed peasant consciousness which Comrade Stalin had gone to such trouble to help the Soviet masses overcome, especially in the gulags. Of course as a German he had no time for Stalin, but as a Communist he was obliged to toe the theoretical line. He embraced the view that eating these foods was not ideologically correct. I might add that this also included turnip, parsnip and swede: loathsome roots, but they still were quite easy to obtain in East Berlin. He had grown up on them but would not touch them now. It was very hard to prepare his meals. Sometimes I would queue for hours for a few limp carrots or some spinach in summer. He liked dumplings made with finely milled wheat flour, and sometimes would accept dried beans or peas at a pinch in his soup.

It goes without saying that what I liked had nothing to do with what we might eat. Although an ardent supporter of the equality of the sexes, when it came to the domestic realm there was perfect clarity. He would choose, I would implement. For example, I am quite fond of pike, which makes a nice dish when served with wild mushrooms and sour cream, but he would insist it be made into a goulash with onions and paprika, and then throw the actual pieces of fish away, leaving only the sauce which he wanted served with fresh bread. I considered undergoing psycho-analysis to try to uncover the reasons why I went along with his nonsense. But go along with it I most certainly did, until that fateful summer of 1980.

I was now 49 years old. I had no children, and so retained a slim and elegant figure. I dressed modestly but well and had a fondness for good quality shoes, some-times obtainable on the black market, as well as nylon stockings and silk underwear. By this stage there was little physical relation between Magnus and myself. Every once in a while I would put my hand on his shoulder or his arm and feel him shrinking away from me which confirmed that I physically repelled him.

It was as if he did not see me at all. Or rather, he saw me, but not as the person I was, but as a kind of object which shared the space of his world in order to meet his needs. If I say he was cruel I do not mean that he deliberately hurt me or threatened me or ripped up my papers or anything like that. He was cruel in the way only totally self-obsessed people can be, because I didn't actually exist for him and this is one of the greatest of cruelties, to be so profoundly ignored.

Imagine my surprise when he told me I was to accompany him to Rovianiemi. If you have never heard of Rovianiemi, neither had I, but it turned out to be the capital city, if such you could call this collection of primitive wooden buildings, of Lappish Finland. A large delegation of theoreticians had been invited to join with local dignitaries and educators for a symposium on the theme: 'Finlandization and Radical Socialism'. I told Magnus politely that I did not have the least desire to go to Finland and especially not to spend a whole week of my life standing around with the other wives or going out on sleighs or whatever one did for amusement in the Arctic North. He was adamant, however. All delegates were required to bring their wives, or they were not permitted to attend. And it was a major honour for him to have been included. At his age, he feared nothing more than the call to the Rektor's office to announce that he had been 'retired'.

Admittedly there were many far worse ways of being 'retired' in East Germany at that time, but he had little fear of the State apparatus, ghastly though it was, because his writing was so highly regarded by theoretical Marxists around the world. I may not have mentioned that he was translated into Chinese, Spanish, Urdu, Vietnamese, and several other Eastern European languages, as well as

Russian and English, although prior to Finland he had never been encouraged, or rather permitted, to travel outside our familiar East Berlin, indeed he hardly travelled at all except once or twice to Leipzig.

What Magnus feared most was being ejected from his comfortable suite of rooms at Humboldt to make way for some younger and more enthusiastic theoretical fellow who happened to have taken the Rektor's eye. I did not think there was any basis for this fear, but old men must inevitably feel something like this no matter who or where they are, as their powers decline, and the cruelties of age come upon them.

Of course I went with him. It was pointless to argue with Magnus. The reason for this flurry of international activity, as one would expect, was political. Finland, although close to Russia in many ways, was independent, or at least it was not declared a part of the Soviet Union. This presented a major conundrum and so far the problem had received only an unsatisfactory materialist explanation. The Taistoists, an important progressive movement, were seeking a theoretical answer to this mystery. The KGB had already put committed socialists into the Finnish universities but this was still not enough. Not to put too fine a point on it, Finland remained capitalist. The politicisation movement had been particularly strong in the South, and it was expected that the International Symposium would be held at Tampere University, but a series of internal struggles resulted in the exact opposite happening, namely, the Symposium was to be held in the very far north where Primitive Communism reigned.

I found myself being conveyed by plane and bus into

the frozen Arctic along with a large contingent of theoretical Marxists and their wives. Rovianiemi wasn't much to look at, stuck in the flat wastelands, but imagine my surprise when we were offloaded onto a convoy of sleds pulled by reindeer, and set off through the snow for the Arctic Hotel which was around 25 miles from the city in the midst of the forest. The reindeer were splendid specimens, tall and graceful and very responsive to the instructions of their drivers, dark round Laplanders with merry smiles and twinkling eyes, as far as you could see behind their furry hoods. They, the reindeer I mean, wore bright blue or orange collars with tinkling bells, and a jolly sound they made in the absolute white silence as we left the flatlands and came into the splendid snow-draped trees. You could smell the purity of the earth as it could be with none of the works of man upon it.

The Arctic Hotel was quite a surprise. A series of low log-walled cabins stretched around a central courtyard where the reindeer sleds pulled up. We were bundled into a large hall with a splendid fire burning in the far corner. Outside the temperature was certainly below freezing, but here it was warm enough to take off our hats and gloves and our fur lined coats. I won't go into the details of everything, because this is not meant to be a travelogue, but soon enough we found ourselves in a dining hall where an excellent meal was served. There was a tasty soup, although it had no vegetables in it. And there was pure Finnish vodka, in large jugs set out in the centre of each table.

I haven't said anything about Magnus and vodka, but I must do so now. Magnus hated vodka, I don't know why exactly, something had happened during his early years, but while he would drink beer occasionally, he never touched the transparent spirit, and neither of course did I. We led a very sober life. But something happened there at the Arctic Hotel. Whether it was the company, the strangeness of being isolated in a place where most of the people were real living breathing Primitive Communists, the anxieties Magnus had been suffering over his position, or something only a psychoanalyst could uncover, Magnus let himself go.

That first night, and the next morning, and at lunchtime and in the evening, Magnus drank vodka. He didn't become falling down drunk or disorderly and he, unlike many of his colleagues, did not engage in fights about theoretical tendencies out in the courtyard, but he seemed to be transforming into a different person. On the morning of the third day he was to give the keynote address on Transition. He drank vodka with his breakfast – they eat a lot of that dried rye biscuit – and went into the lecture room with a large friendly smile on his face, a most unusual and let me say quite terrifying thing for someone accustomed to his normal miserable and gloomy expression.

I wasn't the only one who noticed. His paper caused quite a stir among the comrades. It wasn't the paper he had laboriously written, I know because I had as usual typed it, and where he normally reads from his text very closely, now he simply looked into the audience and spoke in short and clear German sentences. He seemed to be arguing that the cultural ethos arising from the presence of Primitive Communism within the borders of the State presented a very real alternative to the Communism hailed by the Party. Not only that, but it rendered the State itself superfluous.

A large group of students lined the rear of the room. They were Laplanders, who attended the University in Rovianiemi although why there was any need for a university here was unclear to me since the local people learnt everything they needed to know by simply living in such a place. Well, so be it. There were translators in little booths at the back of the hall, and his lecture was being delivered to the Russians and Finns and Laplanders simultaneously.

He stopped speaking with a flourish. The Germans in the audience stared. The Russians leapt to their feet, protesting in very long sentences, demanding an extended discussion period in order to counter his argument. But the Laplanders, to a man and woman, since there were both sexes present although it was hard to see that beneath their strangely decorated clothing, began to clap and cheer. In the midst of the pandemonium a small group rushed across the room and onto the stage. One, a young woman with glossy black hair in plaits down to her waist, seized the microphone and started to speak, in round Lappish vowels, while the others surrounded Magnus, holding onto his arms and stroking him all over. The chairman tried to restore order, but the Russians now began arguing with the Germans, as if they thought Magnus represented a German position, while the Finns who weren't at all sure what had happened opened several bottles of chilled vodka which they had hidden beneath the stage and drank toasts to each other and to Magnus for providing such an entertaining spectacle.

By the time I got to the front of the room, Magnus had

disappeared. I thought the Finns must have taken him off to drink with them and decided to go and find some coffee in the dining room until everything quietened down. I hoped Magnus was not in trouble, but feared he must be, because whatever he had said had changed the tone of the event entirely, and the level of passion remained alarmingly high. I didn't want to speak to him just yet and thought it best to keep out of the way for a bit.

I found some hot coffee and dry biscuits and was walking across the snowy courtyard towards our cabin when I caught sight of Magnus sitting high up on one of the Laplander's sleighs. The young woman who had spoken in the lecture hall was sitting next to him, wrapping soft furs around him, then pulling a thick hat with flaps for the ears down over his head. He was beaming. A bottle of vodka was in his lap, and he was swigging from it. But even more astonishing, in his right hand was what could only be one thing, although I could not believe my eyes – a hunk of dried, dark meat – reindeer meat of course. He was tearing at it with his teeth and chewing away enthusiastically. The young woman was pulling more pieces of meat out of a leather satchel and piling them on top of his furs. She was grinning happily, and took up the reins of the sleigh, shaking them slightly. The beasts, so slender and graceful, shook their heads with their extraordinary antlers, and in a moment the sleigh took off, the bells leaving behind nothing but a merry tinkle which soon faded out leaving only the snowy silence in the courtyard. Behind me somewhere I could hear the buzz of conversation, with the odd excited shout, but clearly the delegates had got over the worst of their surprise and were now presumably drinking coffee or vodka or both.

That was the last I saw of Magnus. He disappeared into the world of Primitive Communism. It caused a stir for a while, but as the 1980s progressed there were other things to think about regarding the so-called revolution which after a few years collapsed though no-one could ever have imagined such a thing.

The local authorities in Rovianiemi investigated and eventually reported that Magnus was living in a remote region with a Lappish family. He had no intention of returning to Germany. Easy going as the Finns are, they gave him some kind of permanent visa. Some years later I received an official letter stating that he had died of natural causes, leaving a wife and young son. There was no will other than the one he had made out in my favour, so I went on living on Warschauer Strasse until the Wall fell in 1989.

I did remarry and my second husband is a chef of international renown. We opened a small restaurant specialising in regional German cuisine, which has been a great success. I look after the menus and do the books. We live a very cosy life on Spandauer Strasse not so far from Warschauer Strasse. Of course, it's all elegant shops and expensive flats these days in the old East Berlin. Who would have thought Berlin-Mitte would become such a fashionable address?

I sometimes see some of my husband's old colleagues. Most were sacked from the University after the Wall fell, since Marxist theory is no longer fashionable anywhere, especially not in the ex-DDR. I am glad for Magnus that he didn't return from Finland. And for myself, too, for if

he had, we would have been living a miserable sorry existence, him unemployed and me depressed and lonely. So
as far as I'm concerned, you just can't beat Primitive
Communism, but I also must credit vodka and reindeer,
for truly these restored our lives.

8

BANGKOK DIAGNOSTIC

Rain falls in October, the gutters fill, the laneways overflow. A sound, a baby crying, or maybe it's a cat on a rooftop. Crunching footfalls on the motel forecourt, is it broken glass or diamonds from Sierra Leone?

Enemies hide everywhere. But who are they? Leaves are shredded, eyes gleam behind the torn gauze of a battered window, the rain falls. Windscreen wipers bang on an old truck somewhere. It looks like a factory, derelict, some distant suburb, nobody goes there, nobody who matters. Slow jazz through tinny speakers and if you shake your head you will hear the news reporters, as usual they blame the crazy pills, the accused is guilty, he'll get off, someone else will pay.

Time passes. What time is it? You don't wear a watch. You've lost your I-Phone. When the rain stops at dusk in a lurid sky a huge screen pulsates at 72 beats per minute, in blinking red, things go better with Coke.

Just look at the figures, they said it was the IMF, globalisation, the financial crisis, now it's something else, nobody really knows, they call it a revolution but nothing ever changes.

On the street kids are out of school, motorbike riders speed by in black helmets with silver anchor-chains around their necks, women and children cry in cardboard slums, there's no money for drink, no money for drugs, try anything, go nowhere, going back for more of the same.

From high above the street it's sudden death, was it suicide or was he pushed? The roads are closed, a symphony of police sirens, megaphones, traffic jams, hostages have been taken. The police look like criminals, the criminals look like police, snipers are in position on the roof, it's a clear shot, is it politics or just a robbery, or are they the same thing?

Up country the Army generals wear golf clothes and order their bodyguards around, it's a minefield and the phones never stop ringing. They drink whisky, they talk, you can hardly understand it, it's some other language, if only that newsreader would shut up. Monks are chanting. His Highness is said to be in Hua Hin. It's like 1932 all over again. Who's behind it? Communists? Capitalists? Fascists? *Farangs*?

Meanwhile the air-conditioning fails, the computer screens flicker, some say ghosts and demons have come up from the underworld. He's a Godless Communist, he wants a Republic; he would be President-for-Life. You can make a bomb in a garage and drink Red Bull in a laneway, but you are doomed regardless.

Out on the river the Thai flag flutters, Land of the Free, long-tailed boats slip between the rice barges. The police move in but don't expect machine guns – Uzis! Too bad, half the cops are dead. The hostages are shot and the assassins speed off in black Mercedes. They were jungle soldiers once, but the city is their playground now.

At the International Development Bank, the charges are set, you can only stand so long on a roof looking at the city through the pouring rain wearing a black balaclava. Leap off the roof, and as you go, pull a rope and a green parachute opens.

It was 1997 that did it. Princes, politicians, bureaucrats and generals, going round in circles dancing *ramwong* in the Royal Park, going round in circles. It's a heady cocktail with their junk investments, empty housing estates, half-built offices. It got worse despite fortunes spent on new Buddha images and diamond-encrusted amulets supposed to change their fortunes.

Through the city the yellow spreads, a vivid butter stain across the overhead railway. Wearing it, not wearing it: you make a statement either way. The red-shirt drivers wear headbands like tribal warriors, they've all seen *Bang Rajan*. Some won't pick up yellows so the crowds push into the Sky-Train, they'd rather not take a *tuk-tuk* anyway. Stinking city streets, exhausted by exhaust, speed, confusion; up here, they can pay and ride high above the city in air-conditioned carriages, down below it was like *Blade Runner*, but now it's November and there's not so much rain.

The newsreaders are never silent. The phones never stop ringing. Fear, fear, the periphery belongs to the devil, the terrorists are in the city, loaded with grenades in shopping bags, keep your head down, keep your eyes down, anything could happen. The Fiend is the saviour of the poor, feeding them Red Bullshit in blank dusty provincial midnights. Western journalists scratch their heads, ring up academics, academics scratch their heads, ring up Western journalists. What happened to the Land of Smiles?

Now they are holed up in Government buildings. No-one can move them. They want 30% democracy. Days of violence: tear gas, beatings, confrontations, the police are back, their crisp brown thighs rubbing together, holsters full to the brim.

October was hell, now it's November. What will we have, a Cabinet Meeting or a coup? Ha, the Fiend has fled. Let's stop the whole country at the airport, we'll party on the tarmac. Desperate honeymooners, what about their bookings, there are no hotel rooms, where will they go? The party is getting louder, that sounds like grenades, that sounds like an Uzi, but then there is singing and laughter and women cooking noodles, scented steam rising into the early morning, bring a piece of matting, sleep anywhere, here are cameras, more speeches, make a comment, grab that redshirt and give him a good dressing down.

Army, police, they are shouting at each other, nobody dares to start it, trigger-fingers itching, imagine, one of those shootouts between the army and the police, seen it at the movies, *Bangkok Robbery*, it would be just like that.

News from the court! The Fiend's stooge is out, the Party's gone, but it makes no difference, they'll just change names, 'Thais love Thais', 'Friends of Thailand', it's the same old gang. They call them fresh elections, but they're as stale as ever. Still, it has to finish, the men in golf clothes work the phones, there must be a way out, a compromise, the tourists have stopped, the economy has stopped, what about the gold reserves, poor country poorer than ever?

And the moon makes a smiley face. That's a sign: let's go, it's December 3rd, that's enough. Export industries damaged. Tourism destroyed. No more supply chain. Can you understand a Thai joke? *Farangs* can't. So, was that the revolution?

They pack up, woks, baseball bats, sleeping mats, plastic bottles, banners, booklets, helmets, they expected more trouble than they got, it's a success, a stand-off.

All the way back to the city it's a yellow highway, to the centre where everything that matters has been mattering for three hundred years, never mind the IMF, never mind the Development Bank, never mind the Asian Finance Agency. On the other hand, don't forget the mobile phone and the Blackberry, crowds learnt how to use them in 1992 and now they are even better, but are they the same crowds, is it the same protest? Who wants democracy? Not too much, thank you. Shift the deckchairs! The King is not dead, long live the King!

9

———————

THE DUM DUM FACTOR

Z APATA: 1989.

Funny thing about the future: you never expect it. You make plans and take steps and think you can influence outcomes but in the end you don't know what will happen. I had one surprise after another. I mean, don't get me wrong, things are all right but life's not how I thought it would be. I could have paid more attention, there were hints so to speak. But I had such belief in myself and my role in the movement I always followed my own path. I thought I was right-on, ignoring anything that held me back from expressing my full revolutionary capacity.

Take this place for instance. When I first got here, I should have realised it wasn't right for my kind of work. But it is unbelievably beautiful. I have always been a sucker for beauty. Seduced by aesthetics, you might say. The rolling hills are capped by rocks like Gaudi sculptures linking earth and sky. Dense bush embraces gullies, rushing waters leap and flow and pour into a sapphire sea. Although I must say I don't like that Dum Dum mountain up there lording it over us.

All this country once belonged to the First Nations people. They basked in the sunshine from the very beginning of time until massacre and disease arrived. That mountain was some kind of sacred place. I can believe it wasn't too pleased to see the white man cutting down its ancient trees and crawling up its sides like ants.

The old way of life has long disappeared but many descendants still live in these parts. In the beginning I reached out. They didn't have a Cultural Centre then, they used to sit around the edge of town or down near the river. I brought them a selection of information sheets. I tried to explain that their people were victims of the international fascist capitalist colonialist conspiracy, and their only hope was to join us in supporting the revolution to come. Nobody disagreed but they didn't seem all that pleased to see me. One fellow said he might be interested but he was a bit busy. Well, I was a bit busy myself.

Everyone said Melbourne was the place. The comrades would welcome me. There was a lot of suspicion in London then. Traitors in different movements spread horrible rumours. I heard a rumour that someone was spreading the rumour that I was a spook. Shocking. As you can imagine, I couldn't trust anyone and it seemed like a tactical exit was the best strategy.

In the Anti-Bolshevik Anti-Revisionist Leninist-Maoist Revolutionary Thought Brigade the struggle intensified beyond our abilities to respond. Like so many others we left the Communist Party of Great Britain due to its moderate tendencies. The Revolution had been so close in the 1960s. The failure to seize the moment in France in May '68 had been an unspeakable betrayal. We held that weak self-important so-called theoretician responsible. I am still writing my book, so I don't want to say too much about it here. But he stopped the Revolution in its tracks. He should have been executed by the comrades but instead he was promoted to the top academic position in Paris where he went on pontificating for a decade until he strangled his wife and that was the end of that. I must keep on with it, but I'm finding it hard these days, especially in the middle of the rainforest with that damned mountain brooding up there all the time.

Crystal Rain: 2015

I don't know how much of Dad's writing was important. What are you meant to do with the stuff dead people leave behind? It might be a collection of China ornaments or some decorative teaspoons or, around here, woven dreamcatchers that have been rotting away on windy balconies for decades. You keep a bit for the memory and send the rest to the Op Shop. Dad left hardly anything useful behind. He had one good leather jacket which he brought from London back in the 1970s, and two pairs of steel-toe boots. He always wore steel-toe boots because they were good for kicking pigs, that is, policemen, and you'd think he had spent most of his time out on the barricades kicking pigs but when I started reading the book that mean lady wrote about him I found out that he had only been in a couple of confrontations and there weren't any barricades in London anyway.

She had a hide, writing about Dad like that. Her book was published way back in the old days, but we never heard about it. I found it wrapped up in plastic in the potting shed. Dad must have put it there, I don't know why he kept it. I don't read much anyway but I felt I should read it since it was about Dad but honestly, I just didn't get what she was on about. I don't go for all that feminist BS, it's such a downer.

Poor old Dad. He kept his boots in immaculate condition and polished them all the time so when I took them down to the Op Shop I knew they'd find a good home. They were way too small for Hemp, unfortunately, he's not exactly a giant but Dad was a real shrimp.

As for the rest of it, the stuff in the basement. OMG! I call it the basement, he called it the shelter. It was underneath the house near town. I could never understand why Mum gave in and agreed to move there. It's much better here at Dum Dum, very spiritual. I'm lucky because my man is useful. We came back and he built a house overlooking the creek and that's where I am right now baking bread and listening to the parrots while the kids are at the community school.

Anyway we had to live in that house a lot of the time and Dad wouldn't let anyone in the basement. As he got closer to the other side, me and Phoenix, Phoenix is my brother, we told him that he had to give us the key because it ought to be cleaned out, rats might be in there. But he'd never let anyone in. He said it was his legacy. He kept the key locked away in a little metal box which he told us was nuclear proof but actually it was just an ordinary strongbox you could buy at any security shop, it had a key code. He said he had forgotten the code but we didn't believe him.

After he died Mum (Ferntree that is, she doesn't like us calling her Mum but I just can't help it), anyway she told us to leave it alone, she didn't want us messing around down there, but then she went on a retreat to India and we thought we should do something about it while she was away. Phoenix finished up hitting the strong box with an axe and we found the key in an envelope so we opened the metal-reinforced door and finally got inside.

It was a big underground room where people in the old days probably played ping-pong or had dirty parties.

Dad wanted the house because of the basement so we moved there and that's where all his boxes and papers and writings ended up. We still spent a lot of time out on the commune. Mum liked to stay with Bikram and his family. They always made room for us. Dad didn't come. He said he got hay fever but it was more than that. He said it was the mountain, the shape of it, the light. I wish he'd told me earlier; I might have been able to explain it to him, the way the ancient power lines run into one another under Dum Dum and join the earth together all the way to Tibet and all the other holy places. But I guess he wouldn't have believed it because he was a scientific materialist.

He definitely did not like our normal spiritual practices. He especially hated the bell ringing for morning meditation at 5.00 am every day. I told him how much better he would feel if he could get into it, but he said it just wasn't his bag. That's the kind of thing they used to say in the old days.

It was a surprise when we found out Dad had bought

that house before we even went to live there. Mum had no idea that he had any money. He must have stashed it away in some overseas bank account we knew nothing about. I suppose he was ashamed, being such an anti-capitalist, so he wanted to keep it a secret.

Honestly, that house was nothing but trouble. There was something wrong with the foundations, there were white ants in the rafters, water came in when it was stormy and half the time the river washed the dirt road away. But Dad was really happy because of the basement. He never threw any of his papers away. He didn't care about material goods, but he kept all these roneoed minutes of meetings, discussion papers, newsletters.

Is roneoed a word? I asked one of the old folks around here, he laughed and said he hadn't thought about a roneo for years, but he knew what it was, and he described it for me and even drew a diagram. I still couldn't understand how it worked but there you go, old school machinery has never been my thing, well, I'm not much good at new school either. So a roneo makes hundreds of copies using purple ink from a kind of sheet that you put into a drum which turns around, it was the only way they could copy things in the old days and that's how they published all their political stuff. It took ages, no internet of course, maybe that's why the revolution never really got off the ground.

Dad brought boxes and boxes of stuff out from England when he came. There were ships then, boats carrying cargo, they would take passengers as well, it took like six weeks or something, can you imagine, but it was cheap and he said it was better than taking a plane. There weren't many planes in the old days and the fares were high. Funny that. Planes are pretty cheap nowadays, but everyone is saying they are bad for the environment.

So he had all this stuff and he said it was to be kept forever, a record of times and events to be preserved, it should be given to a library or an archive and we should make sure that it went to the right kind of place.

I can't tell you how awful it was. A lot of the stuff in boxes got damp after the floods, the bottoms fell out as soon as we tried to lift them up and there was more stuff in plastic bags all over the floor, some of it was all right but something had eaten into the bags. There wasn't any sign of rats but it was insects I suppose, maybe insects have evolved to eat plastic which would be a really useful thing when you think about it, especially if we could learn to eat the insects. Anyway a lot of it didn't seem to make sense so we stuffed it into more rubbish bags and took it to the tip.

There was more in folders up on the shelves. I asked the local library, but they said it wasn't their kind of thing and I should try the big Library in Sydney. I hoped they would take it all away, but they wouldn't even look at it unless I made some kind of index. They wanted original manuscripts, they didn't want old newsletters or whatever. I said I would try to sort through it, but I didn't have a clue what I was doing.

My man Hemp said he was sick and tired of me spending all my time over at the old place. He was pretty dark when he found out Dad had left it to Mum and apart from a small amount of cash I would get nothing. The house was worth a lot more now, even though it was a bit of a wreck. It is good that Mum came back from that ashram in India. She says she'll sell the old place and get a unit by the sea, maybe not Byron, it's too expensive, but somewhere like that. It's great to have her around, I'd never let on but I really missed her.

Zapata: **Memories 2012**

Crystal has been on at me to write down my memories. My 'journey' she calls it, it's another thing people say today that annoyed me when I was younger but now I just let it go. Anyway, she wanted me to write about how come I finished up here on a commune near Dum Dum. I suppose that's a fair question.

It turned out to be much harder than I expected. The comrades in Melbourne said it would be easy. They had the names of a few people up north who were ideologically sound, they'd moved up there a few years before for some Festival thing which they said was their revolutionary moment. I think now that the Melbourne brigade wanted me to go away. It's nothing new, being rejected, so many factions turned in on themselves, I was quite used to it, but still I was a bit disappointed.

One of the reasons I left London was because I got into a stupid thing with a university student. She was very young, like nineteen, and she was beautiful, fantastic looking, girls of that age are pretty attractive no matter what, but she was really something else. She was also incredibly smart and liked to argue the toss about everything. She came from a good middle-class family and hated living in the suburbs, but she didn't have the money to move out on her own. I could see she really wanted to move in with me, but although I was keen on her physical attributes I certainly wasn't interested in cohabitation. I liked it that she admired me, I felt I could teach her a lot which is always a good basis for a relationship with a girl but after a while it became too much. Too much togetherness, too much arguing.

She was persistent though. I couldn't seem to get rid of her. I wasn't paying attention. Can you blame me? There was a revolution to think about! She said I'd be sorry, but I thought it was just girlish petulance. Quite a few female comrades took a dim view of what she called our 'relationship'. I tried to explain that in a revolutionary context men and women were comrades not boyfriend and girlfriend and told her to read *On the Origin of Private Property and the State* so she could see how important it was not to fall into bourgeois thinking.

She read it and then she started arguing about that as well and she wouldn't shut up, next thing she was going to consciousness raising groups and now I was the enemy, me and every other fellow. Of course I believed in equality, but women had to remember they were women. She followed me around to all the meetings and rallies, it was embarrassing. It was a relief to set out for Australia.

It wasn't what I expected, that's for sure. I'd supposed it was a backwater of theory and that the local comrades would be delighted that someone like myself had come to join them. I offered to make myself useful by speaking at meetings and writing summaries of the papers being given at the monthly meetings but after a while they said they didn't want me to speak any more, I had had my turn, and although they had sympathy with the position of the London Anti-Bolshevik Anti-Revisionist Leninist-Maoist Revolutionary Thought Brigade they themselves had moved away from Anti-Revisionism in light of the need for praxis in the contemporary conjuncture.

I couldn't exactly understand what that was. Australian politics were opaque. They didn't seem to follow the logic of British politics where it was obvious who was the ruling class and who were the workers. Workers in England had jobs in coal mines and factories. There were shop stewards and local union branches, and even though they were mostly with the Labor Party they still had some elementary Marxism and understood about the revolution.

But here it wasn't like that. There were plenty of workers, but mostly they didn't even belong to unions. There were a few exceptions, the wharfies and builders' labourers and brewery men. Strikes mostly happened just before Christmas and there'd be a pay rise, and everyone would go back to work. No sense of class unity. Many actually worked for themselves. They were tradesmen with their own businesses. They bought their own houses and mortgages were their main concern apart from drinking beer on every possible occasion especially while burning meat at a barbecue. It was very hard to get anyone excited about domination and resistance.

The only people interested in the revolution were people who hung around the universities. Some were lecturers and some were students, and there were others who didn't seemed to do much at all, had part-time jobs or called themselves artists or songwriters. They were pretty good with theory and read a lot. I couldn't get their 'line' though. There was a lot of loose and foolish thought going on plus a lot of drinking. So going to live on a commune seemed like a good idea.

When I arrived in the north nobody would have me. Some wanted me to pay to buy in – what kind of communal movement is that? Others wanted me to contribute something, like physical labour. No thanks. I drifted around for a while but then I met Ferntree and everything changed. Although she was much younger than me she took me under her wing. She was living at Chakra Cliffs, right under that mountain, with fifteen other people more or less, and she kept the whole show together. She organised things. She cooked lentils and made bread. She was very smart and beautiful in her own way. I was relieved to be able to live in her room, it was nice there, but I didn't really click with the other communards.

It was hard to put up with the drivel they talked. I tried arguing with them. It drove Ferntree crazy although of course she never showed it, she believed in good vibes and hated any kind of conflict which meant she finished up doing everything for everybody else. But I got used to it after a while and I learned how to say the same sort of things they did. I was good at working out how to sound like other people, and once I got onto the weed it was a lot easier, and after the mushrooms it even started making a kind of sense.

We lived on her welfare benefits. I did have some money, but I didn't tell her about that. Then she got pregnant with Crystal, and that's when I knew I would have to do the right thing. Not get married or anything bourgeois like that, but I would have to take care of her. I'd never made a woman pregnant before and it made me feel different somehow, like it was a new phase of life. When that big old house came up near town I decided I'd better buy it. It was a bit out of the way. There wasn't even a proper road, or a name for one.

I thought Ferntree would be relieved to get away from the commune. I promised we could have some other people move in with us so we wouldn't be living like a typical nuclear family, but what with one thing and another nobody stayed for long. You had to drive for ages along horrible roads. The kids had to go to school. We did argue about that. The town school was nearer although the kids didn't like it and in the end they spent a lot of time back at the Cliffs. Somehow Ferntree convinced the authorities that she was home-schooling them. After a while I didn't worry about it anymore. I had my own work to get on with.

Ferntree never paid any attention to money, which I admired. I told her I had sold a book in London and had a bit coming in and otherwise we would live on her Centre-link payments. She thought it was great about the book but never asked to see it, let alone read it. Which is what I had expected. She didn't approve of reading books, said reading was bad for the eyes. I hadn't finished the book, I was still working on it.

The house had a basement. I told her it would be our fallout shelter and I did put some tinned food and water in there, but soon it was out of date. The Melbourne comrades sent all my boxes up and there it was, I had a great place to keep my whole collection.

It was good she didn't like reading because that London girl wrote a book about me. She even sent me a copy, but I hid it in the potting shed. Who would have thought it would turn up again as an e-book?

HELEN V. WORTHY. GEORGE *"ZAPATA" O'Donnell: The Failed Revolutionary*. Kindle Edition, $2.99. 2012.

Author's Forward to the New Edition: In this book, first published by The New Woman Press in 1978, I describe the way political movements failed after the 1960s largely on account of the stubborn refusal of men to change their innate sexist behaviour. This is a personal recollection, based on diaries and notes I made at the time, rather than a politico-theoretical analysis. I have decided to re-publish this memoir as it seems right for our times. Women are finally refusing to put up with patronising self-aggrandising males with their lewd jokes and crude efforts to commit unwanted sexual intrusion onto women's bodies. Readers might think this is something new but believe me it isn't. My own experience is proof of that. The origin of these appalling behaviours may go back into prehistory, but it was the revolutionary sixties that spread them into our collective culture. The things young men got away with then led them to grow into old men thinking they could get away with them forever. There are signs now that those days are over.

The story of George O'Donnell who styled himself Zapata in a narcissistic gesture of futile self-promotion is typical of the young men all over the world who convinced themselves that a revolution was not only possible but imminent. They would be at the forefront of the struggle and leading lights of their movement. Since so many wanted to be leading lights, it meant that there would have to be many movements, and so it came about that the energies of a whole generation of youth were frittered away in tiny groupuscules led by semi-madmen whose main purpose was to demonstrate their own superiority over one another and have sex with any women they fancied without having to take any responsibility.

I was lured into this milieu as a gullible young student. Like many others, I was proud to be the girlfriend of a leading cadre. Zapata was not particularly good-looking, but he had a kind of intensity which drew me, and many other girls as it turned out, to him and kept us there despite our better judgment. It was only after he had fled to Australia that I fully realised the extent of the exploitation I had suffered. Luckily the British movements did not turn fully violent and destructive, there was nothing like the Red Brigades or the SDS or Baader-Meinhof, although I'm not exactly sure why not, since the rhetoric was pretty much the same. Had it been otherwise I might have finished up in jail, or dead.

If you are reading this and you are younger than fifty you probably won't have any idea what I am talking about and maybe you won't even be interested in which case you have wasted your GBP2.99. If you *are* interested there are various historical accounts which will tell you more. All I have tried to do here is reflect on how those years affected me, an ordinary girl from an ordinary English background.

I have always tried to be fair to George. But I feel it is right that I speak my mind and describe how pathetic and misguided the ideals and practices, or *praxis* as they liked to style it, of George and others like him really were. I haven't quoted much from George's own writings here.

There is a good reason for this. It is almost impossible to find them. Apart from a few Newsletter comments which have survived in the London Library he didn't publish anything. He kept saying he had written a book. If he did write it, it was never published. Nobody I know has ever seen it.

His only published piece is a commentary on Louis Althusser's 1966 paper on the Chinese Cultural Revolution, a paper which was until recently only available in French. He said he had read it, but I don't believe his French was up to it. There's an English translation now and I've had a chance to read it properly. I think George completely misunderstood that paper. As far as I can see it supported the Maoist 'revolutionary road' which George also supported so it's not clear why he argued against it. Then again, Mao opted for a massive ideological revolution to sweep away feudalism and since this meant changing gender relations I suppose that was an issue. George certainly hated women in uniform.

Here is how he began:

Comrades, we must never forget the importance of critique. Our brothers and sisters have performed a very useful service in contributing their perspectives to the Broadsheet published here under the banner of the London Anti-Bolshevik Anti-Revisionist Leninist-Maoist Revolutionary Thought Brigade. Their pieces are important for the furtherance of our historic destiny as frontiersmen of the coming Revolution. I recommend you attend to them closely.

My own piece, with which this Special Commemorative Issue begins, takes us to the heart of the contemporary dilemmas of the Left. It is obvious that Louis Althusser was the author of the anonymous paper on the Cultural Revolution in China which was circulated long before his treacherous betrayal of May '68. The misinterpretations within that paper have fed the absurdities now being peddled by some of our female comrades, even those who until recently were part of our own movement.

Who could disagree that women should struggle alongside their male comrades? Who could object to the idea that they should be recognised and rewarded and even take up arms in defence of the Revolution? But does this mean that they should forsake their basic role as supporters of those who by nature and necessity must take the lead? Does this imply that our females should forsake their femininity and start acting like men? Surely not!

To understand the principles of the Revolution we must reject the pursuit of irrelevant goals created by the incorrect and bourgeois thought of those who are unable to accept their biological destiny.

On and on he went, trying to destroy the good work that the sisters had begun under the influence of so many wonderful women thinkers, not least Julia K who had been in the party of French Leftists who visited China. As far as I could see, Althusser was not much interested in 'the women question' and did not consider it at all relevant for the analysis of social formations through subjection to ideology. It certainly didn't inhibit him from strangling his wife.

I tried to persuade George to read Julia K's works on women in China, but he was simply incapable of rational discussion. We fought about it all the time and finally I left him as I should have done long before. Julia K explained things which nobody else had thought to explain. Most feminists focused on questions like who should be doing the photocopying or making the tea or looking after the children. Those were important things, but these other issues were more profound.

George refuted everything. He said there was no need to go beyond the original texts of the revolution. He had read every single word of *Das Kapital* and *The Communist Manifesto* and said these explained everything very clearly. He agreed with Engels that women were subordinated because of feudalist legacies in capitalism but the logic of this in relation to his opposition to feminist thought made no sense. It took a long time for me to understand this. Like many others in our Brigade I had believed in him absolutely.

In this book I aim to illuminate the futile struggles which went on around Theory at that time. But more than anything I want you, the reader, to see how easy it is for girls and women to be duped by men into acting fundamentally against their own best interests. I believe my book is especially important because it is high time that young people recognise what the real revolutionaries, the feminists of the 1970s, were up against. Young people must forge ahead despite the deluge of anti-woman propaganda, idiotic cultural demands and outright violence which continues to be directed against them by personal and collective representatives of the Ideological State Apparatus. Althusser was right about that at least.

Zapata: 2013

I went to the doctor today and got my test results. I don't want Ferntree or the kids to know about it, but I guess I'll have to tell them soon enough. I'll have to make a will. There's only one thing I really care about. It's just as well we never had to use the shelter. I would have sworn that there'd be a nuclear war but so far, no luck. If it happened now, it would be a damned nuisance because there's no room in the shelter because of my collection.

Yes, I've been adding to it. I started going through the notes toward the books I was going to write and found the ink had faded, so I started copying them out again. I could have typed them but for some reason the older I got the harder I found typing and although Phoenix had tried to help me work one of those confounded new computer things I just couldn't get the hang of it. It was strange because somehow a note which was about two pages long turned into ten pages by the time I'd finished rewriting it. There was so much more to say about everything than I had said at the time.

The things that I thought back in the 1970s – well, they weren't wrong exactly, but they didn't match up. I could see there were warnings all along the way: about the bourgeoisie, about capitalism, about women and the rest of it. I was trying to explain how nothing had gone according to plan. It was hard, especially when I'd had a bit of a smoke. I started writing other things, which I'd never done before. Creative, a few bits of memoir. It was very hard to keep track of my writings because the filing system I'd set up when I first started multiplied inside itself so there were a lot of headings and subheadings and more subheadings underneath those because I kept on trying to explain what I had been thinking when I wrote whatever it was in the first place.

I don't really mind about dying. I hope it won't be too painful. If I can just sit here on the back veranda having a few tokes it shouldn't be too bad. I really hope I don't have to go to hospital.

I don't even feel like the same person. I look at photographs of myself in the London days. I'm proud of those newspaper articles showing me leading the march on May Day. I'm carrying the banner. That was quite a day, I finished up in the cells, but they let me go the next morning, which was disappointing.

I'll leave the house to Ferntree, she deserves it. I haven't got anything else, except the collection. That won't be worth anything in money, or I don't think it will. Crystal and Phoenix will take care of it, I've told them often enough how important it is. For the future, I mean. You must know about the past to even have a future. It is so hard trying to think about time and history and what is really happening. I can see how much easier it is to shut up and do nothing.

I've got a bit saved up, I'll split that between them. Really, I'd rather leave it all to Crystal, she's a bit daffy but she's been a good girl, a good daughter. Now she's pregnant again she'll need some extra money. But I can't leave poor Phoenix out. Ferntree thinks I don't know about that night up at the Cliffs, but I saw them together. You can see right away where Phoenix came from, but you don't talk about that kind of thing here, because everyone is equal, and if I'm with Ferntree then her kids are my kids kind of thing. Which I do approve of.

It's too late now to publish my book on Althusser and the sixties. Anyway all these other youngsters have started writing books about him. I found a couple of reviews; they seem to have got it right. I guess it doesn't matter if I don't say my piece now. It's just another thing I should have done years ago. But I couldn't really, not up here. And it was great to be with Ferntree and to feel safe at last, where nobody would persecute me.

True, you still must be ideologically correct. I've learnt that the important thing is to know when to keep your mouth shut. Just keep quiet and nod your head, agree that things are getting worse and worse, frogs disappearing and so on.

Nobody knows who I really am, or what a big role I played in the revolutionary movement. They don't even seem to know about revolutionary movements anymore. A lot of people thought that going back to nature would be enough, living peacefully in tune with the environment. You still have to put a lot of energy into it. And regardless of what you do things go on getting worse and worse, and now Mother Nature's really had a gutfull.

It's hard to do anything here, nothing ever happens because the weather is too good and everyone is stoned all the time. Which I guess is what Lenin meant about people being infantile, but in the end, maybe it's not such a bad way to be. Now I must get ready to start dying. I've had it pretty good really. It's funny that, I ignored all the warnings, and nothing went the way I expected but it's turned out all right in the end. So I'd better go and make a pot of chai.

CRYSTAL RAIN: **2017**

It is hard after someone has passed over, like there is a lot of processing going on and you need to go easy on yourself. I had to get rid of most of Dad's stuff in the end. I kept a few of his hand-written letters for old times' sake but I did find this one big plastic box with its lid on tight and that's where I found a lot of the writing I've been putting together here.

I thought it wasn't fair that so little of Dad's work had survived and nobody would be able to remember him or what he stood for. The main thing they would read would be that London woman's book and that didn't seem right. I hadn't understood a word of it when I tried to read it the first time, except that it said horrible things about Dad. Even though he was a silly old crank he was my dad, and he did love me in his way. He loved me more than he loved Phoenix, but I'm pretty sure that's because he knew Phoenix wasn't his actual biological child although Mum never would have told him, but it's something like a sixth sense with men, you know, it's like they just can smell it if the kid's not theirs. Like lions or is it baboons, what do they call it, pheromones?

So I started reading her book again, I bought it for my Kindle and although I know the Zon is part of the exploitative transnational capitalist machine I read a lot more these days. You can download whole books for a couple of dollars or even for free which is a weird way to run a capitalist business but anyway it's good for the customer and it's quite interesting reading them. Hemp won't let us have a TV, which is OK, but it's made me keener on reading than I ever was before although I'd really like to get audio books but they're so expensive.

That woman spent a lot of time going on about Dad's negative views on women, feminism, women's liberation. But that was just a part of it. The real issue was French theory. I didn't know what that was, or even that there could be a kind of theory in French which would be different to one in English or in Russian for that matter. But I knew there were two people Dad wrote a lot about. One of them is that French dude. The other one is this Russian guy Vladimir Lenin. I tried to get their books in the local library, but the librarian couldn't find them anywhere except in some University and ordinary people aren't allowed to borrow those books. I thought I'd ask old Pete, because he'd been around the traps in the old days and he knew a lot.

It was interesting what Pete said. The reason that woman hated Dad so much was because of how he was a typical Old School revolutionary man. At first the women supported the men but then they worked out they weren't getting much out of it; they were still followers and not leaders and it wasn't fair that their sexuality was oppressed and they were supposed to have orgasms on demand and were still expected to cook dinner. And there was another lot who were against him too, men and women both, because he stuck up for Lenin and that was against their party line.

Revolution has to mean liberation. And Lenin just didn't get that. Plenty of things he said were right on, but he was such a hard-liner and had a big problem with plea-sure. You can tell it by looking at his photos. He hardly ever smiled. He reckoned people like us, well he didn't know us of course but all the young people in his day suffered from an infantile sickness.

Lenin was against having fun. That was it basically. All these young guys and girls back in 1917 or whatever it was thought revolution would be a party. Lenin and his thugs put paid to that idea. He said to be a true revolu-tionary you had to wear boring clothes and be grim all the time. It was because of Lenin that the anti-fun brigade had taken over Communism and caused all the bad vibes like the Gulag, mass persecution, starvation and that type of thing.

Communism as an idea might be the right one. From each according to his means and all that. But it turns out not to be so great in practice as we found out on the commune. When the ones who had stuff gave it to those who didn't it empowered the freeloaders who wouldn't lift a finger to help themselves. This was one reason why Mum was okay with moving away. But things changed and by the time me and Hemp moved back here there were new rules. People must look after their own places now and have their own money and do their own cooking, which is a relief.

And I think Dad was right, if revolution depends on the working class then you have to have a working class and in recent times hardly anybody is working class any more at least in countries like the US and Britain and Australia because everyone who isn't filthy rich works for Centrelink. All the actual jobs have moved overseas where people are happy to work for practically no money and make all the junk people think they need like cheap clothes and television sets and toasters and electric toothbrushes and – well – everything really. Even cars. And people in the advanced countries pay heaps to buy them since they have forgotten how to make them themselves.

The ones who own the big companies and their children and grandchildren go on getting richer because once you've got capital it makes more of itself, and that means you can buy more places and build more buildings and real estate goes up and up and nobody can afford to live anywhere anymore.

We're lucky to have land on the commune. We grow a few veggies and have great parties. I suppose we're a bit infantile, or at least some of us are. I'm out weeding in the hot sun all day while Hemp smokes dope on the veranda. Just like Dad, really. But I don't mind. I'm glad because I think Dad was happy in his last years. He realised Mum was right: in the end the revolution has to be inside your head, and he was still trying at least.

TROPICAL SURGERY - A NOVELETTE

On a bright Sydney morning Louisa Pignolet stepped out of a limousine. At home she had admired her Carlos Falchi sling-backs. White with red trim, they looked great with her tailored suit. She turned back and forth in front of the Louis Fourteenth gilded mirror (a reproduction of course, but still). Now she had to teeter along the narrow streets of the legal district to locate the right building and her toes hurt.

People hurried by in dark suits and white shirts, purposeful and busy. She walked up and down twice before seeing a narrow entry door and a discrete name chiselled on the granite fascia. There, that was it: Emilion St Jacques, Avocats. Louisa had never visited Pierre's lawyers. If documents had to be signed, he brought them home and she did as he told her because she trusted him completely. Whatever else he was, Pierre Pignolet was a thoroughly reliable man who had never misled her or lied to her or let her down. Now he was dead.

Inside the lobby a special elevator led to the upper floors. She pressed the glowing gold button and felt the smooth rise upwards. Her coiffure had been disturbed in the turbulent air so she smoothed it back as best she could, surprised by the lingering scent of the product the hairdresser had used. Before, she would not have allowed it. Pierre did not like her to wear what he called "cheap scent", least of all the slightly decadent commercial products she liked. It was annoying but understandable, given his role as Managing Director (Asia-Pacific) of his family's famous cosmetics company.

Louisa caught sight of herself in the reflective surface of the lift. She thought of the words 'a woman of a certain age'. Yes, she was over fifty and menopausal. Her face was plain, she was overweight, jowls were developing at the base of her jaw and a tracery of wrinkles ran around her eyes and across her forehead. No amount of super-expensive creams and lotions had been able to hold back the sagging skin around her neck. She looked away.

The elevator slowed gently. She stepped out onto thick carpet. A spectacular vase of flowers occupied a carved and polished hall table. Someone behind a frosted glass door must have pressed a button because it swung open so she could enter. A beautiful girl sat behind a desk. Her long nails tapped at one of the latest computers, her lovely cheekbones highlighted by the faint blue light.

She looked up and smiled politely.

'Good morning' she said. 'Welcome, Madame Pignolet. Monsieur Lascelles is waiting for you. Let me show you through'.

She came around from the desk and Louisa was

almost sick with envy at her lovely figure and long legs, clad in black seamed stockings. What a look! She was more like a model than a secretary.

A tall, elegant man came forward and took her hand. For a moment she thought he would kiss it, but instead he shook it gently and then gestured at the leather chair into which she was obliged to sink.

'Madame Pignolet, my sincere condolences for your loss'.

'Thank you' she replied. She never knew what to say, especially since such condolences were rarely sincere. Here at least they pronounced her name correctly. As they should do, specialising in European legal matters especially wills and estates. Pierre had announced that she could have absolute confidence in this company regarding his post-mortem affairs. Little did either of them expect it would be so soon.

'May we offer you coffee? Tea? Sparkling water?'

'Coffee please'.

'Miss Fontaine?'

The beautiful secretary or assistant or model, whatever she was, murmured and left the room silently.

M. Lascelles opened the embossed files on his desk.

'Dear Madame, I do not know to what extent you are familiar with your husband's intentions. I will assume we are beginning *ab initio* if you understand me'.

'As if I know nothing? Well, Mr. Lascelles, that would be true enough. Pierre kept his business affairs highly confidential. As for his will, he merely told me I would be well provided for'.

'Indeed, you will be' replied the lawyer, smiling benevolently. 'Your late husband has left a significant estate, and the greatest part of it goes to you, apart from some modest legacies'.

Miss Fontaine returned with steaming coffee and slipped away.

'Perhaps if you will allow me to summarise. Your husband's estate comprises three elements. In cash and shares, approximately two million Australian dollars equivalent. In real estate, there is the house in Hunter's Hill which is yours as his widow, valued recently at over four million dollars. I believe he has already gifted you substantial items of family jewellery including diamonds and precious stones, currently held in safe deposit. And there is a quantity of gold bullion deposited in an Australian bank, to the value of over five million dollars.'

Louisa gasped. 'Gold!'

'Yes, not unusual especially in European estates, although there may be taxation questions regarding its source. As far as I can see, your late husband inherited the gold from his own paternal grandfather. How it came to be deposited in an Australian account is another question. But as there are no inheritance taxes applied under these circumstances, I foresee no problem other than one of extensive paperwork. You need not concern yourself about it, the accountant who deals with the Pignolet business will assist.'

She sat silently, digesting this information.

'No doubt you will want to know about the distribution of the estate. There are small legacies for each of your late husband's nieces and nephews, some seven in all, each of $300,000. There are two philanthropic donations of half a million dollars, one for cancer research and one to support scholarships for Australian art students to study in one of the Paris ateliers associated with the Pignolet family. The remainder of the estate is left to you'.

The lawyer smiled again, a little wolfishly. 'With your agreement, your husband directed that our firm continue to represent you legally and manage everything associated with the granting of probate in NSW. I trust this will be satisfactory?'

'Yes, absolutely satisfactory. But how do I get access to the funds?'

There was already a lot of money in her cheque account. Somehow it appeared every month without her doing anything. Would this just go on? How would it work? What if she wanted extra money for something, say to buy a new car, or some clothes?

She outlined her concerns. The lawyer was calm and patient, even though she seemed to know so little about money and how it worked. He explained as clearly as he could, told her to make an appointment with the accountant, reassured her that all the complications would be dealt with by him personally and ushered her out of his office with gushing politeness.

She had not ordered a limousine to take her back to Hunter's Hill. She thought she might walk through the city and browse in a few of the expensive shops with the imported brands. But to buy something she would have to try it on, and she dreaded the supercilious glances of the beautiful girls who graced the hallowed halls of commerce at this end of town. She knew they would despise her expansive thighs and rounded, not to say bulging, abdomen. She hailed a taxi instead and went home to the beautifully renovated kitchen where she made toast and vegemite and gazed at the sparkling harbour. She decided that as soon as she could she would do something about herself. She needed a complete change. Nothing less would do, especially now she was so very, very rich.

SOME MONTHS later she arrived at Sydney Airport in another black limousine. The driver fetched a trolley, removed two suitcases from the trunk, opened Louisa's door, and ushered her out with a routine smile. She wobbled on her new Jimmy Choo peep-toes. She didn't need to pay, it was already taken care of, but she took a twenty dollar note from her wallet and slipped it into the driver's hand. He looked somewhat grateful but not quite grateful enough, maybe Louisa had not given him the kind of tip he was used to. How do you know these things if you don't do them every day? Pierre always took care of that kind of thing. It was too late now to offer more. He gave her a slack salute and got back in the car.

Louisa thought there would be porters to wheel the trolley to the check-in desk, but everyone else was pushing away so she would have to do the same. The suitcases sat snugly side by side and she laid the matching carry-on bag on top of them, swung her handbag over her shoulder and marched onward.

She went to the Business Class desk. Louisa liked Business Class. She and Pierre always used to fly First together but now it was her money she did not want to appear flamboyant. Anyway, Pierre had always said First Class was a security risk for a woman travelling alone.

The everyday people lined up for the flight to Bangkok at another desk. Their singlets, ghastly tattoos, rubber thongs, board-shorts and pudgy waistlines made her shudder.

Louisa took her passport and confirmation from her handbag and handed them over to the girl. Or was she a woman? Everyone looked so young these days. She was told to put her bags on the conveyor belt. They were heavy. She didn't know how long she would be in Bangkok; it could be quite a while. And she wanted to have the right clothes. She didn't know if they would still fit after everything was over but she wanted to look her best. She heaved them up.

The girl smiled as she looked at the passport.

'Good morning' she said. 'To Bangkok today? Just a moment'. She peered at the computer screen as the labels printed then attached them and made the bags move along.

'You haven't printed your boarding pass?'

She seemed slightly annoyed. The computer had asked if she wanted to print her boarding pass before she came to the airport, but she didn't think she had a very good printer. In truth she hadn't been sure exactly how to do it. Pierre had managed the new technologies; she was only learning.

The woman looked at her with an oddly vivid glance. She must be wearing coloured contact lenses. That was an idea. She hadn't thought of that, certainly her own eyes had become a bit dull, a muddy green-brown. Pierre had called them emerald once. He said he was drowning in them. Always partial to exaggeration, Pierre, but in that sexy French accent it was charming and almost made up for the thinning pale hair on his rounded skull and the pouches beneath his slightly globelike eyes.

They had had some good times together but really it was a blessing that he went when he did. When you marry a man twenty years older his departure can't be much of a surprise. Although it was a bit spectacular in the dining room at the Excelsior Hotel on their wedding anniversary. His heart stopped while he was eating rillettes. Which she hated, the smell, like hospitals and nursing homes, which she had had more than enough of when she had to work in the pre-Pierre days.

Then she heard the words she dreaded.

'There you are, Mrs. Pig-nollet, your Boarding Pass through to Bangkok'.

Louisa didn't protest. What would be the point? She had protested a thousand times, but it never made any difference.

Always the same, 'Mrs. Pig-nollet'. Despite her newly abundant resources, she hadn't been able to do anything about it in time for the scheduled trip. Once again, she felt deflated, annoyed, diminished, disgraced. When she met Pierre she hadn't realised how Pignolet was spelled. The way French people said it was fine. 'Bonjour Madame Pinyolay' they said, and it sounded quite pretty really. But with Australians it caused confusion and, when she told them how to say it properly, they were mystified.

In the Motor Registry, at the doctor's surgery, every time she had to give her name it was the same: 'Pig-nollet' they called. 'Mrs. Pig-nollet' cried the spotty youth behind the counter. 'Number 548, Pig-nollet, go to desk 12'.

'Pin-yo-lay' she would say when making an appointment. She knew their next words. "How do you spell that?' 'P-I-G-N-O-L-E-T" she would reply. "Oh" they would say, "Pig-nollet".

She had leapt at the chance of marrying Pierre but soon wished he had a more alluring name. Beauchamp or La Marche would have been better. She wanted to change her name along with her body. It turned out one was easy and the other much harder.

Her birth certificate didn't correspond to a name on any record. Her mother put down the name of the man she said was Louisa's father, a Dutch name, van der Veer, who was he? Her mother called herself Mrs. Boyd. Mr. Boyd was her mother's grandfather. Louisa vaguely remembered him or thought she did.

Now she wanted a new name but didn't know what to choose. Maybe she would find out after she had her surgery. Meanwhile, her paperwork completed, she walked on her too-high heels through Customs and Immigration and into the Luxury Lounge where she found some magazines and drank a little champagne.

IN THE BACK of one of the magazines she found an advertisement for Madame Hirshey's Psychic Services. Not long after Pierre's death she had visited Madame Hirshey. She poured out her story, she couldn't stop, it was such a relief to be heard.

When she was young, she had to work to support

her sick mother who suffered from nerves but really it was the gin. After her mother died, she began to work for a private agency and then Pierre hired her to care for his ailing mother and she went to live in the amazing waterfront mansion in Hunter's Hill. She was a kind of servant, but she loved it there. The jacarandas bloomed, the gardens were rich and abundant, there was a cleaner and a cook, all she had to do was look after the old lady who had dementia and hardly spoke a word of English.

Pierre was the soul of generosity. He looked neat, prosperous, well-dressed, his suits and shirts were hand-made in Hong Kong. But then the old lady died. Louisa thought her luck had been too good to be true and was looking for another position when Pierre surprised her with a proposal of marriage. Why? He said he loved her, but she didn't believe him. They had only been married a few years and now suddenly she was a widow. What awaited her? What would happen next?

Madame Hirshey read the Tarot, did her astrology chart, and consulted her Spirit Guide, an American Indian named Big Cloud. All signs pointed in the same direction. Unconditional love awaited. Louisa had to travel far from home to find it. Where should she go? To the East, said Madame Hershey. You mean, east of Australia, or the Far East, or what? Madame Hershey said she could not tell her that, only that her destiny lay in the East. She should listen to her dreams.

Dreams? Louisa hardly remembered her dreams. But one morning she woke with the strangest sensation of peace. There was a sweet scent in the air. She had been walking in an oriental landscape where golden statues lay on the ground and glittering towers clustered high in the air. Where was it? She had no idea.

That very day she was leafing through a magazine and there was a two-page spread discussing the merits of a cosmetic surgical vacation in Thailand.

She examined the before and after shots. It was weird. The women in the pictures still looked the same, but so much better. That young girl on the left was pretty but her chin did recede quite a lot. After surgery her chin aligned with her lips and nose. And maybe the nose itself had been adjusted a little. Below was a woman wearing a pair of droopy panties. Her hips and thighs bulged with complex landscapes of cellulite. The same woman in the photo on the right – you could see it was the same woman from the butterfly tattoo above her hip – was smooth and shapely. Those thundering thighs were completely gone and the panties were lacy and elegant.

She started doing research as best she could with her limited abilities on the Internet. It was a revelation. The many clinics in Thailand offered anything you could want, breast augmentation, tummy tuck, facelift, vaginal tightening, labial bleaching, you name it.

There were reviews on Tripper Help. Hundreds, both men and women, had done it. Sure, there were a few problems. Someone had died while having their buttocks lifted. Someone else complained of shameless greed because their surgeries ended up costing around the same as they would have in the US or Australia. But money was not a consideration for Louisa. She wanted it done, and quickly.

Sitting at her kitchen table in Hunter's Hill she read that the surgeons at the Great Superior Hospital in

Bangkok were the best in the world. They had learnt their skills operating on complex microsurgical cases. Apparently Thai women sometimes cut off their husbands' appendages if there was a mistress in the picture. The surgeons could re-attach the organ, provided of course that the wronged wife had not thrown it to the chickens, or was it ducks? She wasn't sure she believed this, but it didn't matter, as long as the surgeons were brilliant. And unlike the Western clinics, all the operations could be done at the same time. There was no need to go for a tummy-tuck one week and a nose job a month later. The Great Superior Hospital offered a single, extended stay including recovery in a luxury hotel attached to the hospital for as long as required.

They could re-create a body to order. It might seem selfish and self-indulgent, but so what? Louisa knew what she wanted. She wanted a new partner, a proper one this time, one who would love her in the way she needed to be loved. That meant she had to be beautiful. Pierre had loved her in his own weak way, but the passion just wasn't there. She couldn't blame him, though, how could he have really loved her when she had so many imperfections?

AT THE GREAT SUPERIOR HOSPITAL the stay might be days or even weeks, depending on the procedures. She would have a personal concierge, a trained nurse who would be with her throughout the whole process. If she had to go to Bangkok to make herself ready for her new life, she would. She sent emails, they sent emails back. Everything was arranged, and now she was handing her boarding pass to the flight attendant – a cute young guy, as it happened – and as she did so she said very clearly: 'I am Madame Pignolet. Pignolet, that's right, Pignolet'.

'Certainly, Madame Pignolet, let me show you to your seat'. He said it perfectly the first time, but would he remember? She sat quietly and sipped champagne. Sydney twinkled as the plane banked high into the clouds and wheeled away towards the north. Soon, no more Mrs Pignollet. She would be the beauty she was meant to be with her true love at her side at last.

IT WAS A SMOOTH FLIGHT. She went through immigration and customs. The official looked at her passport and then at her and then at the computer screen and then at her again. He was entirely expressionless. Thailand was supposed to be the Land of Smiles, but not at this desk.

Retrieving her baggage, she wheeled it outside into the viscous air. There were buses, taxis, cars, people shouting, scurrying about. Her feet hurt terribly after eight hours in the air. She had forgotten that the air pressure made them swell. It had been hard enough to get her shoes onto her feet again, let alone push a trolley. Someone was supposed to meet her. Men in dark clothes stood behind a railing. She scanned the line. One of the men was waving a sign above his head. It was the worst ever: Mrs Pig Nollet in big black letters.

There was nothing for it but to go over to him. He took her suitcases and motioned her to stand further down from the other passengers. What now? What if he stole her luggage? What would she do? She hugged her handbag closer to her and thought she might not be able to breathe. Then she remembered: she had money. She had credit cards. So what if he stole her bags? She could go and find a taxi and ask to be taken to some expensive hotel. There would be a Hilton or a Marriott, and she could buy new clothes. They might even be better. She had the address of the hospital and the name of the doctor, she could go there tomorrow. Whatever happened she would be fine.

She had started to look around for the taxi line when a cream Mercedes pulled up and the same man hurried over.

'So sorry Madam have a problem sorry again parking traffic ….' Or she thought he was saying that but anyway it didn't matter because she could see the name of the hospital on the side of the car. He helped her in, she was enfolded in glorious air-conditioning, given an iced cloth for her face and hands and a bottle of cold mineral water. The car pulled out and soon they were speeding along in the dark night, through a city that looked like something from a feral video game.

In the steamy air neon lights marked tall buildings and overpasses. Women wielded huge ladles and shook woks over blue gas flames while customers clustered around tiny tables. She could almost hear them slurping.

The car windows were tinted so nobody could see inside. She felt safe, a chrysalis about to undergo its transformation. If she had had someone to discuss it with they might have changed her mind. But there was nobody who cared, nobody at all. She could do anything she liked. The freedom of it made her feel dizzy. She rested her head on the scented leather seats and closed her eyes.

The hospital was also the hotel. Smiling attendants met her at the luxurious entrance and after check-in she found herself in a large room full of fresh flowers, fruit, a bar-fridge with juices and waters, chocolates and alcohol. She showered, changed into her nightgown and switched on the plasma TV, flipping between the various cable channels. She thought she should try to go to sleep, but she had snoozed already on the plane and it was only eight by her body clock.

A printed program on top of the television folded out into several sections. One whole channel was devoted to romantic comedies so she watched Hugh Grant and Julia Roberts in *Notting Hill*. She couldn't imagine she would ever look like Julia Roberts no matter how much surgery she had, and would she even want to? There was something scary about that huge mouth with its enormous teeth, they looked as if they might snap you in half. Still, everyone agreed she was very beautiful.

Finally she drifted off. Early next morning a slender girl appeared with a tray of fresh fruit, hot coffee, and toast. From the window she could see the hazy skyline with its hundreds of towering buildings glinting in the morning sun. What a place! There were more papers in an envelope to fill in, then a phone call to say she would soon meet the medical team.

She showered again and dressed, pulling her hair into a French knot. Soon a girl in a white uniform appeared and led her into a hushed corridor. Elegant displays of flowers stood in nooks along the polished timber walls.

Once through the folding doors it looked more like a hospital. She sat waiting in a scented room, reading the information pack with her name on it. The operation would start the following day, meanwhile they wanted to check all her vital signs, take bloods, measure her every which way, take photographs, consult about her preferred outcomes, look again at the pictures she had sent of herself, younger, at the person she had once been. The person she would become again, but with many improvements.

Two nurses came into the room. She had to remove her clothes and wear a hospital gown but even that was elegant, made from Egyptian cotton. She submitted to whatever they asked. She was giving her bodily envelope over to its new phase of existence. Her surgeon Dr Pattana appeared, and introduced her to his assistant, to the anaesthetist, to the head nurse. And then to Nurse Sipapornchai, her private surgical concierge. She said to call her Nurse Sippy. It sounded ridiculous, like some children's soft drink, but who was she to object? Every-thing was so well organised.

The doctor gave her an injection. He said it would relax her. There were pills to take as well. It was impor-tant that she eat nothing after midday, and drink plenty of fluids but only until evening. Nurse Sippy led her back to her room, turned down her bed and helped her get into her night clothes. Smiling gently she left, and Louisa was alone.

She felt her entire system shutting down, she was warm, she was relaxed, she didn't care about anything. Her past life, all those faces, the dead and dying in the nursing home, her poor mother, her husband with his nose in a plate of rillettes, those calling her name, "Mrs Pig-nollet, please come to the front desk", all of them drifted away as if they had never existed. There was only herself, and the new life she was going to experience because, despite everything, she was alive, she was healthy, she was rich, and soon she would be beautiful.

She had never felt so calm and safe. Time ticked away. She vaguely watched old movies with Audrey Hepburn, Cary Grant, Humphrey Bogart and Lauren Bacall, movies her mother had loved. She stood at the window, looking down on the people like ants below, she was floating in the present, no past but a wonderful future.

Something had been pressing down on her. Miraculously it had been lifted and in this light and airy condition she thought of what she had been missing all along. Love, that was what she had been missing.

She stretched out in her cool luxurious bed. Without love there could be no completeness. She had felt it a little with Pierre at the beginning but mostly she felt more like his pet, a sleek furry pussycat he liked to stroke at night. He never really saw her. He presented her with delicious foods, as he might give his cat a new brand of expensive cat food. Indeed, that was what had caused those fatty deposits on her hips and thighs which the doctor's assistants had taken so much trouble prodding and measuring yesterday, was it only yesterday?

Once he was thoroughly used to having her around, he seemed to withdraw and together they were like a nicely wrapped up package, empty inside. They managed to lay in bed together at night for years without their bodies touching except when he wanted sex, which strangely enough he did go on wanting. She didn't mind, it was part of the deal.

Drifting on the satin coverlet, the city unheeding in its bath of steamy air, she watched old black and white lovers gaze into each other's eyes, touch each other's hands, make sacrifices ... oh, those scenes in *Casablanca*, Humphrey's hunger and adoration, Ingrid's limpid gaze, the moment when she turned and the pain burned him as she walked to the plane which would take her and her husband away to freedom, leaving Humphrey behind to a cruel fate at the hands of the fascists. That was love, with its pain and power and compulsion. Even if it ended badly it didn't matter. She needed love to enter her own secret spaces and make itself truly at home. She had never had that kind of love. She craved it.

THERE WAS JUST one moment when she had doubts. She had woken while it was still dark, as dark as it gets in Bangkok, although down below on Sukhumvit Rd it was never dark. She had forgotten where she was. She had been dreaming of the racing cars roaring past at the Mount Panorama circuit when she was with Eric, long-dead Eric who she once thought she had loved, although at sixteen is it even possible? Her poor mother had been so angry about sexy Eric with his motorcycle boots and leather jacket and then he rolled over at 120 miles an hour and went through a hoarding into a plate glass window, decapitated.

Standing in her Bangkok bedroom she caught a glimpse of her body at a strange angle, a three-quarter view. Although her abdomen was a bit bulgy and she had the beginnings of a double chin, she didn't look so bad. She walked into the lavish marble bathroom and took off her nightdress. Yes, there it was, the lighting was gentle but now she could see, standing straight in front of the mirror, all the flaws and bumps and soft bits which had crept up on her body.

She knew then it had to be the right thing. They would transform her while she was unconscious, abandoned to their scalpels and suctions and inserts. Some websites had warned against these methods. They said it was dangerous, that surgery needed to be limited, spread out over weeks or months. Of course, they were just trying to get more money. The doctors at the Bangkok hospital were not subject to hidebound bureaucratic requirements. No matter how long the surgery took she would be treated with the latest internationally accepted methods and afterwards she would be kept sedated as long as necessary for her to be healed.

She realised she was feeling very thirsty and opened the minibar, but all the drinks were gone, and she remembered that she mustn't drink anything now, she would soon be in surgery.

So she lay down on her bed and whatever miraculous sedative they had given her took over and next thing she knew she was being roused by Nurse Sippy, who helped her into her hospital gown and put her in a shiny wheelchair and pushed her out along the silent scented corridor into the lift. Up they went to the surgical floor, a rush of whiteness and bright lights. They even gave her some dark glasses to cover her eyes. So thoughtful!

She caught glimpses of people coming and going, nurses, doctors. Everything was sparkling clean. Quiet classical music played in the background. There were other cubicles around hers and women came past in wheelchairs. Nurse Sippy took her to the toilet. She was dehydrated but managed to provide a little sample. Her bowels seemed to have stopped operating altogether the previous day. Something in the drugs they were giving her? Or just a lack of food? Anyway, it was fine, she didn't want to eat, she wanted to be thin.

Doctor Pattana – Dr Pat – came in to see her.

"So Mrs Pig, all ready now for operation?"

'Please call me Louisa'.

'OK, Mrs Roo-ee-Saa, all ready now for operation?'

She nodded, watching his smooth golden skin reflect the light from the neons in the ceiling, a beautiful man. Let them call her whatever they liked; it would all be over soon.

IT WAS hard to wake up. There were people chattering away in their impenetrable language. Someone was patting her, she was hooked up to tubes and drains, her body felt completely disconnected from her mind.

'Mrs Roo-ee-Saa, wake up now, time to wake up'.

The face leaning over her didn't look happy. Louisa shut her eyes again and drifted off. Where was she going? She had no idea, there was no her, there was no time, there was no place to be …

Next time she woke up there were more people clustered around her bed. Machines were beeping, there was a mask over her face and oxygen going into her nostrils. Something was wrong. She couldn't work out how to ask what had happened. She was drifting back to sleep when Dr Pat bent over her and looked deep into her eyes.

'Please Mrs Roo-ee-Saa, please come back to me now,

can you hear me talk? I am talking to you? Here, see my hand? How many fingers?'

Louisa smiled behind her mask. He really was a lovely man, she could smell beautiful perfume coming from him, from his shiny black hair perhaps, or his skin. She should make an effort. She opened her eyes wide and tried to remove the mask, but someone held her hand firmly and she could not move.

'All right now, here, watch my hand'.

Her eyes followed his movements.

He was speaking to someone else, others in the room. She had no idea what he was saying. She went back to sleep.

When she woke up again there was nobody nearby, just the machines beeping, and the mask was off her face. And she began to feel something terribly weird, as if her body had detached itself from her. She thought about how people when they are dying hover above their bodies and look at them. Was she dying? She tried to look down, but she couldn't see anything. Still, it didn't feel like her.

Then there was pain. It was rushing up and down her nerves, she could feel it going into her head, her brain, then rushing around her arms and across her body and down her side. There was a terrible sound, and she wished the person would shut up as she found it quite offensive, she shouldn't have to listen to it, but then she realised it was herself and she was moaning.

Nurses appeared, there were lights and scuffling and then something went into her arm and everything went away again.

It seemed to go on forever, this coming awake and then

being put back to sleep. But bit by bit she was able to connect with her surroundings. She was not in the same room, there were only a couple of machines connected to her and the acute pain she had felt whenever she woke up had abated to a dull ache all over her body. There were thick bandages and a drip continued into one arm, then they moved it to the other side, then into her hand. Her wrist was dark, bruised.

Dr Pat came in to see her every day. He was always smiling, smooth, elegant.

'Is all OK Mrs Roo now? You are feeling better?'

'What happened? Am I alright?'

'You are very all right dear lady. A little panic for us for a while, blood problem, but we fill you up again and now all good'.

'What about the operation?'

'All success, everything perfect'.

'I still have pain. I can't eat.'

'Ah, no food yet but you have tube in your stomach for your lunch and dinner'.

She couldn't believe she hadn't felt it. After he went, she lifted the covers and moved her hand down and there were tubes in her abdomen. Next time he came she asked him about them.

'Yes, and also we must drain fluid. And you know, after lipo, when you can stand up again you must wear a tight corset. But not time yet'.

As Louisa became stronger she realised there were other women nearby. She could hear them moan and cry out in the night, and new arrivals would sometimes scream. But the nurses scurried in and filled up their drips or gave them injections. Louisa had begun looking forward to her injections. Afterwards she felt happier than she had ever felt in her life.

ONE MORNING LOUISA was woken by Nurse Sippy and told it was time to get out of bed and stay up for a while. They had taken the catheter out and somehow she had been moving her bowels even though it was on a bedpan, the most uncomfortable thing she had ever imagined. But her stools were very soft and afterwards they wiped her carefully until she was very clean. And she had been having sponge baths twice a day where there were no bandages.

'And today we take bandages off face. But please not to look in mirror Mrs Roo, not yet'. Nurse Sippy laughed merrily.

And indeed, when she managed to stumble into the bathroom the mirror had been covered up, a thick piece of gauze taped across it. Did she want to see herself? Everything seemed to be so swollen and bruised. There were bandages around her forehead and neck. She balanced the drip and managed to sit down to pee. There was tenderness in her thighs and abdomen, but it was no longer giving her agonising pain.

Back in bed she asked Nurse Sippy what day it was.

'Oh, now today she is how you say English Sunday?'

'Sunday? But I only came into hospital on Thursday'.

'No that was another Thursday, past time'.

A past time? How long ago? But she couldn't get Nurse Sippy to tell her the date. She didn't have her watch or mobile phone. They had taken everything away, locked it all in the safe. Could she ask for it back? The idea of trying to explain made her tired all over again. She took a white pill and slept.

But at least now she was able to eat. They brought in trays with cool drinks and sandwiches and little bowls of fresh-cut fruits, papaya and melons and strangely scented things she had never seen before. They were so delicious. She had never enjoyed eating fruit so much in her life. They gave her rice with chicken and soup, and little vegetable things floating in a kind of cream. Everything tasted delicate, nourishing but bland.

They had moved her into a different ward that morning for clinical examination and served her lunch there. She was just licking her fingers after some sticky rice custard when the curtain stirred and a face peered in.

'Hullo there' she said. 'How you doing?'

It was so long since anyone had spoken to her in a way she understood that she burst into tears.

'Can I come in?'

Louisa waved her in and reached for some tissues.

'I'm Sharon' the woman said. 'You are Louisa?'

'How did you know?'

'I saw your name on the sign outside'.

'Oh, OK'. Louisa was still sniffling.

Sharon was a tall woman – well, girl or woman, Louisa couldn't tell, she was swathed in bandages. She came to the bed and sat down gingerly.

'Do you mind? Sorry, can't stay on my feet for too long. Still hurting. How are you going?'

'I don't really know. I suppose I'm all right. How long have you been here? Since your operation I mean?'

'Not sure. They don't want you to think about time here, until you are much better'.

'How much better?'

'Until you are able to walk around and sit on a regular chair. When you are ready they will ask you to go downstairs and eat in the dining room. You must get dressed in your own clothes. They are taking my bandages off today, and after that I should be ready to go down. They do it here, in this observation ward, in case anything goes wrong. Maybe you'll be having yours off as well'.

She made it sound like it was a kind of debutante ball. Well, in a way it was, because the patients were going to be revealed with all their bruises and stitches for the first time.

'Wish you could come with me. I feel a bit nervous. Shouldn't be, I suppose, but I won't be a pretty sight'. Sharon touched her face gingerly. Her eyes were deeply embedded in dark and swollen flesh.

'Then if you're still doing OK, you go back to your own room, you know, where they put you when you arrived. I think I'll feel a bit lonely there. I like having people around'.

Louisa wanted to be friendly but wasn't sure if Sharon was right for a friend. It was her voice. People in Sydney could tell a lot about somebody as soon as they opened their mouth. Where they had gone to school, their background, their likely income, where they lived, their place in the social hierarchy. Louisa was well aware that she herself was a complete fraud. Her mother had made her learn to speak properly. Nobody would pick her for what she really was. Sharon? She too probably came from the Western Suburbs. Should she share confidences with

Sharon? She felt woozy a lot of the time from the relaxants. She didn't want to make an inappropriate connection, say too much, even though she would like a pal to talk to.

There was a sudden bustle and burst of excitement. Someone was being wheeled in. Her face was covered in light gauze bandages but as the cluster of nurses and orderlies slid her over into a waiting bed Louisa could see that the patient was a Thai girl, not over twenty. The covering slid back and thick glossy hair around her fine forehead peeped out against dewy skin the colour of pale honey. There was non-stop fussing and exclaiming and chatter around the bed, with folded hands and bowing and scraping.

'Suay, suay' one of the staff kept repeating. The rest echoed. 'Suay, suay' they breathed.

'What's going on? Who do you think that is?'

'I don't know. I'll find out. I can talk Thai a bit'.

'Really?' She wanted to ask how this was possible, but Sharon raised herself from the bed and was slipping out through the curtains. She went over to the desk and hovered, unnoticed.

The group around the figure dissolved eventually and a nurse said, 'Yes please Mrs Sha-Lon, can I help you something?'

Sharon said a few words in Thai to the nurse, who replied volubly. They seemed to be chatting for quite a while. She came back into the cubicle and rested against the bed frame.

'Well, that is interesting. That is Miss Thailand, or maybe it's Miss Somewhere-or-other in Thailand, I couldn't quite get it, but she is going to be Miss Thailand one day soon, that's what they say. She has a royal title, some kind of Princess. Anyway, she is super famous because she is also a pop singer, everybody loves her, and she starred in last year's hit television show. It's like 'Days of Our Lives', it's the most popular show on the telly here'.

'So how do you know all this? Do you live here?'

'Yes, my husband is in condos. We're here half the year. I won't stay in the hot season but it's not bad the rest of the time. It's pretty good actually. I have a housekeeper and a maid and a gardener and a driver. We live in one of the gated estates, near Nakhon Pathom'.

'So why is she in here?'

'She needed some work. Eyes and lips, boobs. The Thai beauty queens all have their eyes done so they look more European. They have gorgeous legs and bums, but their breasts are too small'.

Sharon seemed very well informed. And rich. People make a fortune overseas, expatriates, she had heard about it, but this was the first one she met.

'So you live half the time back in Australia?'

'Yes, the children are in boarding school there. Well, Tanya is in Switzerland, finishing now'. She paused. 'It's a funny life'.

Louisa was interested.

'So how come you speak Thai?'

'Well, I don't really. But I think if you are going to live somewhere you should at least know a bit of the language'. She laughed. 'I know it's not a popular view. Most of the expat wives can't be bothered'.

Louisa thought about this. She had tried to learn French for a while, but Pierre laughed at her.

The noise in the room died down and Miss Thailand

was left alone. But not completely. Men in suits came in occasionally, checked, then went back outside. Later that night Sharon told her there were armed guards out in the corridor. There was a lot of violence in Thailand over politics and money. Anything could happen. Louisa decided it would be good to talk to Sharon even if Sharon wasn't the kind of person she would have chosen for a friend. She felt so alone here high above the city with her aching body and itching skin and nobody to call on the mobile even if they'd let her have it.

THEY DIDN'T TAKE her bandages off. Dr Pat looked and said she wasn't ready but they wheeled her back to the hotel room. Strange sensations passed along her skin, crawling feelings like tiny insects. Then there were sharp pulls as if something was tugging at her from the inside. Nurse Sippy came by twice a day. She was longing for a shower, but this was complicated, as the elastic bandages holding her newly flat flesh in were hard to remove and Nurse Sippy said she was not ready yet.

But she was getting better. She was told to walk around the room and up and down the corridor whenever she could. Soon she was pacing around half the day, between the dainty meals and drinks wheeled in on silver trays and the movies and TV shows on the cable channels. There were news channels, BBC News and CNN but they played the same stuff repeatedly and were so boring she couldn't pay attention.

Nurse Sippy appeared very early one morning, took her into the clinical room and told her the bandages were coming off. It happened quickly, there was no problem, and she was taken back to her room and told to take a shower and go downstairs for breakfast. At first she felt weak and uncertain but as the lovely hot water splashed over her body and she was able to wash her hair properly and walk around the bathroom and towel herself dry she felt so much better.

Nurse Sippy had uncovered the mirrors and told her to look at herself. It wasn't too bad. There were bruises and dark patches along her jawline and a kind of yellowish purple around her eyes. Her belly was so much smaller, and the pads of fat around her hips had gone. The thighs didn't look much different, but the skin certainly seemed smoother and although there were dark marks where the lipo thing had gone in. The skin was already healed over.

While she was showering her bed had been made and Nurse Sippy had laid out some of her clothes – a pale cream linen skirt and white pin-tuck blouse, and a pale lemon cotton cardigan. It took ages to dress and Nurse Sippy had to help put the elastic corset around her middle.

'You happy?' asked Nurse Sippy.

'You know what? Yes, I am really happy' Louisa replied. 'It is fabulous. Great. Thanks so much'.

'Thank you too. Well, it not me, it is Doctor, but all good now, yes?'

'How much longer until I can leave?'

'You go home? Or go holiday?'

Louisa had noted that all kinds of pleasant holidays were offered when you had finished the surgical recovery. There were spas in the south on the Andaman Sea, and mountain retreats in Chiang Rai, and luxury river cruises. But she didn't want to be a tourist by herself. She would come back and visit later, after she had met her new partner. Her psychic hadn't made it clear where exactly she would meet him.

'I will go home'.

'Your family waiting for you?'

Louisa imagined for a moment what it would be like to have a devoted family full of loving relatives. It would be amazing not to be so utterly alone.

'No' she said, 'I have no family'.

A strange expression passed across Nurse Sippy's smooth oval face, something like pity. It didn't matter. Louisa had paid her bills, had her surgery, she was going to get on with her life and there was nothing now to stand in her way, at least once she had her name changed.

She wondered if she could put on makeup, to cover the bruises, but Nurse Sippy told her no, it was too soon, her skin needed to be clean, and breathe. It made sense. She found her Jimmy Choos and stood up in them. Her feet were still swollen. She looked at the ballet flats and thought they might be better, but no, if she was going out in public for the first time, she would look her best.

Nurse Sippy walked her to the lift and wished her a happy day. After breakfast she would be able to take a walk around the hotel or sit in the lobby for a while. She couldn't swim, of course, and it wasn't a good idea to go outside, but there were plenty of shops in the arcades around the hotel, she would be able to go shopping. She picked up her little handbag, not that there was anything in it but she had a handkerchief and some lip balm and a notebook and silver pencil, and her American Express card. That would do.

When she walked out of the lift she was overwhelmed. A vast lobby opened up with an atrium full of palm trees, thick carpets, wafts of perfume, gleaming fixtures and a huge wall-hanging sparkling with jewels, showing the King addressing his subjects on top of some mountain. At points around the room men in uniform stood to attention. Some of them wore what looked like army uniforms. Several were carrying rifles.

A tiny girl in Thai classical dress approached, her hands folded together under her chin, her head bowed.

'You please follow me to breakfast room'.

Louisa found it hard to walk on the carpet in her high heels, but she was determined to hold her head up and walk gracefully. There was so much artistry here. Everything was displayed, arranged, polished. They passed through double doors and into a large dining room set with gleaming glasses and cutlery. Outside was a lush tropical courtyard full of orchids and mini waterfalls.

People occupied most of the tables, some with marks of surgery on their faces, others presumably their friends or partners. There was an air of quiet pleasure. The hostess led her across the room to a large table set for two.

'Please to sit here' she said. 'Will bring coffee or tea?'

'Tea please'.

'Yes, and so please to choose from the buffet'. She gestured at the elaborate table which stretched along the entire wall. People were wandering about holding plates, ordering omelettes, selecting pastries, fresh fruit, pouring juices. It was overwhelming. Louisa wasn't sure she was even hungry. She chose some fresh fruit and a pot of yoghurt and walked back to her table. Damn these shoes. She should have worn the flats.

A silver tea pot had appeared on her table. She sat down, moved the sprigs of purple and white orchids, moved them back again. She needed to rest a moment, suddenly very tired.

She was pouring her tea when a flurry disturbed the placid silence. Through the double doors came a stunning young woman, carrying a small basket in one hand. She was followed by several men in dark suits and sunglasses. Everyone in the room stared. The staff immediately bowed low and gave the classic greeting gesture, hands together in front, bending low from the waist, eyes downcast.

The young woman walked directly across the room and paused at her table. Out of the basket peeked a tiny dog with long tufts of hair on its ears. They seemed to have been tipped in gold.

'Please may I join you?'

Louisa was astonished. She recognised the young woman, the Princess from the hospital ward. She, the Princess, was wearing long floaty panels of glittering cloth arranged into a kind of tight skirt and overshirt. Without waiting for an answer, she placed the dog in its basket on the floor beside her. One of the men in dark suits pulled her chair out and inspected it briefly. She sat and extended a beautifully manicured hand with long golden nails.

'How do you do' she said. 'I am Phra Ong Chao Ying ….' She rattled off several incomprehensible syllables. 'But you may call me Miss Princess'.

'Mrs Louisa' she replied, feeling the soft skin holding her fingers a moment. The accent was hard to follow.

'Please excuse me' she began, after a small sip of water from a crystal glass, 'but I am to improve my English. I am not study oversea but only here in Thailand. My career, I must speak English more often, television and then travel if Miss World'.

'I see'. Louisa smiled at her, and she smiled back. The men in dark suits melted into the background. She had never chatted to someone like this, whose beauty was so overwhelming, although a few tell-tale bruises were visible on her face and neck.

A waitress appeared with a large tray. She bent down at the table and handed the tray up from a kneeling position on the floor, something which seemed almost impossible in the long tight skirt.

The Princess's breakfast consisted of boiled rice with egg, plates of fresh fruit carved into stars and petals and an assortment of tiny pastries. Another waitress approached with a smaller tray. It turned out this was for the dog. She laid down a white starched cloth and placed two golden bowls on it, bowing to the animal after lifting it from its basket.

The Princess ate a few morsels, sipped at her water, and began to ask Louisa about her surgery. She didn't seem all that interested in the answers. Louisa wasn't even sure that she had understood what she was saying. She felt profoundly embarrassed, and couldn't eat anything herself, she was so afraid of dropping it down her front or getting food on her teeth. A Princess... how did you chat to a Princess?

The dog had finished its breakfast and tried to leap

onto the royal lap. She waved a finger in the air and one of the men in suits appeared, put it back in its basket and moved it away.

Another woman appeared carrying a silver coffee pot and fine china cup. After placing them on the table she dropped to her knees and somehow managed to shuffle backwards before bowing and walking backwards away from the table.

Everyone was staring at them. The Princess began to ask about Australia. She said she had heard it was very beautiful. 'Kangaroo' she said, laughing, making little gestures with her hands.

Louisa felt desperately embarrassed. The effort of smiling was making her face ache. She nodded and smiled while the Princess talked. The longer she talked the more incomprehensible it became.

Finally, the Princess seemed to have finished her breakfast. The wait staff appeared bowing before her and made a kind of arcade so she could leave the table. The guards in suits stood around her.

Louisa thought she should stand up too, to say good-bye. She held out her hand. At that moment came the sound of crashing glass, cries and shouting outside the room, more crashing and then what had to be gunshots. The door burst open and men in black uniforms wearing masks and caps poured into the room.

IT HAPPENED SO FAST. One minute they were about to shake hands, the next everything was chaos. Guards rushed forward and pulled guns from under their coats.

The Princess dropped to the ground and tried to crawl under the table. It was obvious she had been wounded. Blood was coming from her neck. Louisa tried to get on the ground beside her although it was very difficult because of the lipo corset. But she managed and reached for the white linen cloth where the dog's breakfast had been served. She folded it quickly and pressed it over the neck wound.

The Princess seemed strangely calm. Her lovely glistening eyes looked at Louisa as she crouched above her. Then she felt someone pulling at her leg and dragging her out from under the table. It was one of the guards, trying to get to the Princess. She heard her own voice shouting at him to leave her alone. Without the pressure from her hand on the cloth there would be nothing to stop the blood. Luckily the bullet had not hit an artery.

But the pull on her leg was too strong and she felt herself being dragged out. Gunfire continued; the noise was deafening. Then she realised she was being pulled towards the buffet table. Many people were sheltering there, shouting and screaming, shaking. Several of the staff were lying bleeding or dead on the floor.

Louisa now crawled along. People pushed at the doors but they would not open. Bullets continued to fly. The guards were shooting at the gunmen, bandits, robbers, whatever they were. Louisa had to find another way out of the room. She pulled off her shoes and began to crawl along the edge of the buffet table until she reached the entrance to the kitchen. The door was shut but she pushed it open and crawled through. Several others were following, they were on the kitchen floor. She kept going and suddenly came to another door, half opened. There was a laneway outside. She stood up and ran forward and suddenly she was in a dark courtyard behind a main road, and there were cars stopped and people running and the sound of sirens approaching. She looked down and saw she had blood all over her skirt, but she couldn't be sure if it was hers or the Princess's.

From behind there were more gunshots and then she was being pushed forward by some of the men in black and she saw they had the Princess too and were half-dragging half-carrying her out the door and then they were being hustled into the vehicle followed by two armed men and the door was sliding closed and they were being driven away at high speed through the Bangkok traffic.

The Princess was holding the bloodstained napkin to her neck but she was no longer bleeding as much. She sat on the bench seat beside Louisa. Her skirt had torn a little but otherwise she seemed undamaged. Her face was pale, but her expression was completely calm, as though none of this had anything to do with her.

The men in the back of the vehicle were completely silent. From the front there was a crackle of static and a torrent of voices through a walkie-talkie. At first sirens came from all directions, but as their speed picked up and they swayed from side to side the sounds diminished and soon there was nothing but ordinary traffic noises.

The Princess took Louisa's hand and pressed it firmly.

'Do not be afraid' she said. 'You will not be hurt'.

'But why have they taken me?'

'They think you are my companion. They think they will get a good money for you, you a *farang*'.

'But what about you? What will they do to you?'

'They think to sell me to some other people. My

father's enemies. About some business they are not happy, lose money, revenge. Now I think we go to some private airport'.

Louisa had never been so terrified in her life. Her heart pounded; her pulse was racing. Yet something about the Princess's calm was catching. She could hardly imagine that something like this could happen to her, yet it was happening, right now. She smelled her own fear, but the Princess smelled like orchids.

After half an hour of rapid travel along a tangle of roads and they left the city. The sun gleamed through dirty windows. The men sat completely silent, holding their guns across their chests, as the vehicle swayed and shook up and down.

'We go west' said the Princess at last. 'To Petchaburi I think. To jungle'.

She had removed the bloodied napkin. The bullet had just grazed her skin.

'Do you think make scar?'

'No, or maybe very small one. You are lucky! They could have killed you!'

'No no, Mrs Louisa, not kill me, have no value dead'. And she laughed a tinkling little laugh.

The road had become rougher, and they seem to be headed uphill.

'We go towards Burma border," said the Princess. 'Might be Burmese army'.

Louisa was becoming terribly uncomfortable. She needed to pee badly. The lipo corset was cutting into her stomach, pressing on her bladder. What if she wet her pants sitting next to a Princess? How humiliating!

Then there were sudden sounds, the scream of brakes

as their vehicle came to a stop, and more gunfire from all sides. The men guarding them called out to the men in the front, but a hail of bullets suddenly shattered the front window.

'Lie down now' said the Princess, pulling Louisa onto the floor.

'What's happening?'

'I think we are rescue. My father's army'.

The back door was thrown open, and uniformed men poured into the van. Their captors were dragged out onto the dusty road. One tried to run away into the jungle, but two soldiers took aim and shot him. He fell into the bushes.

The Princess took Louisa's hand. They stepped down and saw several jeeps stretched out along the road. As the Princess appeared, the men kneeled and bowed. A helicopter approached from the south.

A man in military uniform spoke to her respectfully. He gestured several times at Louisa. The Princess smiled gently and took Louisa's arm. 'Please now to wait for your rescue monks. I go for helicopter ride back to my father's palace. Phra Lokha Dhamma people are taking care of you. All good for you. Go with them. They will save you from the bad men. They are helping you all the way'.

'But Princess … are you all right?'

'Oh very good thank you' she said. "Goodbye now and good luck to you'. A uniformed man opened the door of the black van and Louisa saw the little dog with the gold-tipped ears yapping excitedly. The man wai-ed low to the Princess, who turned with a smile and waved her fingers at Louisa. Their elaborate manicure was intact.

A moment later another black van with tinted

windows appeared through the dust and pulled up next to her. It had a golden logo on the side, 'Phra Lokha Dhamma Foundation' written in English script below the tantalizing obscurity of Thai.

A man in a different uniform slid out the door and took Louisa's arm. He bowed politely then pushed her inside which hurt rather a lot. She hoped her stitches had not been damaged. Then she was sitting on a bench seat clutching her handbag. Two other men sat opposite, and in the front was a driver and three monks in orange robes wearing mirrored sunglasses. The driver backed along the rough country road and turned around. Soon they were speeding away towards a distant mountain range.

Louisa felt increasingly weak as the vehicle bounced and rattled. She tried speaking to the two guards, but they didn't respond. One smiled and bowed, the other was looking out the back window and held his gun on alert.

'Hullo, hullo there' she tried calling to the monks in the front seat. Gold amulets dangled from the front of the cabin, glinting in the sunshine. She thought she might cry, but nothing happened. She was aching all over and terribly thirsty.

'Hullo, can you hear me? Where are we going? What is happening? I need a drink. Do you understand?'

One of the monks leaned down, turned around and handed a bottle of water to the guard and said something. The guard handed her the water. It was cool, covered with droplets from an icebox of some kind. She opened the bottle and drank from it.

'Thank you' she said. 'Where are we going?'

But the monks continued to ignore her. Suddenly the van swung off the unmade road and the rattling stopped as they came onto smooth paving which stretched into the distance ahead.

They were in an upland area, with small gardens in the midst of uncleared jungle. She looked down and saw she was bleeding. Her wounds had opened. At the sight of the vivid red spreading across her clothing she began to lose consciousness and slid down the bench-seat onto the grubby floor of the van.

WHEN SHE AWOKE she was lying on a stretcher covered in soft white sheets. Ceiling fans turned lazily. The air was cool and refreshing, slightly scented. Her handbag was on a table beside her and her clothes were folded underneath. At the far end of the room several patients lay in bed, clusters of visitors sitting around them or on the floor nearby. She was aware that she hurt, but it was somewhere dimly far away, and maybe the body she was lying in was not her own.

Time passed and she fell asleep again. Later, it was almost dark and small lamps had been lit around the beds. Two women with shaved heads wearing white robes were shaking her gently.

'Please Madam lady wake up. Can you wake up? It is time to have food and drink'.

She tried to move but it hurt more. They gently held her body and helped her sit, supported by white pillows. The wooden shutters which served as windows were open to the outside.

'What is happening? Where am I?'

'Here please to eat something. Our doctor will come and talk to you soon'.

One of the women placed a bamboo tray on her lap holding a bowl of rice soup and some fresh-cut tropical fruit. A steaming mug contained herbal tea which smelled delicious. She was terribly hungry.

'Thank you, thank you' she said. 'But please tell me where I am'.

'You are at jungle meditation temple' said the older of the two women. Her English was very good.

'But where?'

'Here is near Baan Mae Kha Salao Yai' she replied.

'But where is that?'

The woman laughed. 'So sorry but cannot explain. Doctor and monk tell everything to you. Please relax now and sleep'.

They left the room, their bare feet hardly making a sound. The visitors at the other beds had gone, and the patients were sitting cross-legged, eating their food. She did the same. It was delicious, delicate and nourishing. She put the tray aside on the small table next to the bed and realised she needed to use the toilet.

There must be a toilet here somewhere. She slid out of the bed, wincing. She was wearing a loose gown over her bandages. She shuffled to the end of the room and saw a door with the image of a woman on it. She pushed it open and found a squat toilet, a bucket of water and a plastic dipper.

She had no idea what to do. She had never seen a squat toilet before. It was just a hole in the ground surrounded by a footplate. There was a hose with a handle and a covered bin in the corner. People must squat down over it but there was no way her knees would be able to manage that. It all seemed too hard, but then the urge to pee became so overwhelming that she hitched her gown up, and let the urine go. It splashed all over her feet and onto the floor. Afterwards she washed her feet and then tried to wash her hands, but there was no soap and nothing to dry herself on.

She shuffled back to her bed and lay down. Surely this couldn't be a hospital. How could she endure it? What if she needed to empty her bowels? It was unthinkable. She would have to get out of here as soon as possible.

But as she lay down, she felt herself drifting away again. Maybe it was something in the herbal tea, but her senses felt heightened, as though she could hear every scrape and squeak from the trees and leaves outside, every tiny movement of birds and animals, the gentle breathing of the women now asleep in their beds.

Next morning it was barely first light when she woke to find she had visitors. One was obviously the doctor, in his white coat with a stethoscope around his neck. The other was a very serious looking monk, in robes of an unusual dark red and thick reading glasses.

'Good morning Madam I am Doctor Somchai Kittibun and this is Phra Ajarn Chah Rangsi. We welcome you to our meditation retreat'.

The doctor greeted her, and she found herself making the 'wai' in return. The monk merely nodded his head.

'We are sure you have many questions, and we will try to answer them. But there are some we cannot, and you will have to trust us'.

Louisa felt slightly dizzy, but her body did feel better. She sat up higher in her bed.

'Am I all right? My wounds ...?'

'Yes, you are going to be all right. Such terrible things to do to a body, but the skill of those Bangkok doctors is great, and you will recover soon. I have inspected and dressed all your wounds yesterday when you arrived, sadly without consciousness. Fortunately you are a strong woman and have revived well'.

'Please tell me what has happened? Why am I here? I need to go back to Bangkok, I need to see my doctors'.

'Unfortunately Madam that is not possible. The Hospital is closed due to the attack. It is too dangerous for you to return to Bangkok just now. Those who tried to kidnap the Princess believe you are also a worthy victim and since they failed with the Princess, they are now attempting to locate you and hold you for ransom'.

'Me? Why me? I have done nothing!'

'That is true, but it does not matter. They know you are a very wealthy woman in your own country. They want to capture you and hold you hostage for payment. Wealthy westerners in trouble in Thailand give them much of their finance'.

'But how would they know all this about me?'

'Sadly, dear Madam it is not the first case of this kind. You have submitted all your personal information to the Hospital through the computer. There are many ways that information can be obtained. We believe it was no accident that you were seated with the Princess that morning. Someone at the Hospital has been working with Mai Fai Sawang.'

'What is that? Are they terrorists?'

'Not as you would understand it. They are a kind of

terrorist in Thailand though. Very powerful, working in secret, they want to remove freedom from our country'.

'So what can I do? Can't I just leave?'

'When you are more healed, yes. But it would be very dangerous for you. They know your passport and your identity, your name and birthday and all your details. You would have to make a booking on an airplane, and get to Bangkok, and get to the airport. And they have powerful friends everywhere, even in the police and the army. We can help you get to Bangkok if you decide to leave. But recommend not so soon'.

Louisa sat baffled. 'How long until I am healed?'

'Perhaps not so long. Maybe one month to be safe to travel. We can give only limited medicine here. We use natural remedies, jungle plants and so on, not so fast to work. You can go to another hospital, but they could easily find you'.

'How long would I need to stay?'

'We are not sure. There are growing forces against Mai Fai Sawang. The Princess's father is a very powerful man. He is our great supporter. He and others are planning to eliminate our enemies, but it will take time'.

'So what? I can stay here?'

"If you wish to stay here, we can make that happen for you. This reverend monk will explain. Now I must attend other patients, I must return to the main hospital this afternoon."

'Where am I? Where is this place?'

'A distant province'.

'So it is far from Bangkok?'

'Yes, but not so far. I will be visiting again in a few days. The nurses here will look after you well'.

'Should I sign anything? Pay you? How will I get my passport? My other luggage and papers? My mobile phone?'

'Please relax yourself. Our friends at the Hospital have already retrieved your belongings. They will be sent to you shortly. You are free then to make your own decisions. But now, I am sorry, I must go, soon my transportation will arrive'.

He turned and left the room. The monk stood away from her bed. He began to speak.

'Please welcome to our Buddhist order. This is very private meditation temple. You are welcome to stay here for as long as you need. But you must obey the rules and undertake training. There are some other foreigners here at this temple and you must agree not to tell them your story, and to remain out of contact with the outside world and respect the rules of retreat. That way, our enemies will not know you are here, and we can keep you safe until you are able to return, that is, if you choose to return'.

'Do I have to pay? I have no money now, I mean, I have nothing here with me'.

'We are not concerned about money or payment. You should not be either. When it is time, your wealth will be waiting for you. You will give us whatever you wish'.

'But I can leave if I want to?'

'Yes, you can leave at any time. You are not a prisoner here. As you choose. But first, you must heal your wounds and get stronger. As time passes, you will learn what you need to know. You are safer here than anywhere. Even the Abbot of our order will help to teach you. We will begin our learning when you clearly see your path.'

Soundlessly the monk turned and disappeared from the room.

Louisa felt exhausted. She lay back on the pillows and heard the swishing sound of a broom, the twitter of birds, a distant fragment of chanting or perhaps it was a song. She closed her eyes a moment and then the nuns appeared at her bedside with more hot soup, eggs and vegetables, and steaming tea. They smiled, bowed, and slipped away almost before she registered their presence.

She ate and lay back on her pillows. How could she decide? Everything was out of her hands. Her life had been taken over. She could not understand it but felt an overwhelming relief. The rightness of staying here hit her. That was all she needed to do, just to stay here and see what happened. Although she would have to work out how to manage the toilet.

FIVE MONTHS LATER.

Before dawn the first birds twittered. Monkeys cried, scavenging around the temple. Dogs barked in the distance, near the fields. Bells rang to mark the time.

She sat up on the thin mattress. She was glad she had a cot, sleeping on a floor mat would be difficult. Her body still twitched and shivered in odd places. The holes where the lipo needles had gone in were swollen and itchy.

Her thin white robes hung from a nail on the wall, near her towel. She took them and trod carefully down the narrow staircase to the shower-room. Four cabins shared the shower, but she was alone this morning. She usually showered under a sarong. Everyone was carefully modest here.

Today was an important day. She felt apprehensive. Also, hungry. She was glad to feel the flesh falling from her, but maybe it had gone a bit far. Bones had started poking from her hips and when she looked down her thighs seemed spindly and uneven, without cellulite but lumpy. There would be no food until after the meditation and then she would have her private audience. She had become used to feeling hungry. It was just a feeling.

She walked along the narrow path through the luxuriant vegetation. Everything smelled fresh and sweet. At the cabins higher up the mountain someone was sweeping swish, swish, swish, a steady rhythm.

It was an amazing place. They had moved her to this temple about six weeks before. It took her breath away every morning. The path led to a long vista of green grass. At the far end the main stupa glowed in the first morning light. When the sun rose it reflected from the burnished dome straight into the closed eyes of the meditators, so they would see the red blood coursing through their eyelids, the network of tiny veins. Already hundreds of people were sitting in white robes, facing the rounded dome. They sat in ordered, neat rows, the same distance apart from each other. Closer to the stupa the saffron-robed monks formed circles radiating out around it.

At this branch temple there were a few hundred in residence, although at weekends and on Buddhist holy days the crowds thronged in from the nearby towns. She had not yet visited the main temple but the endless video loops playing in the meditation hall showed thousands and thousands seated in neat rows facing an enormous chedi, like a golden spaceship, with its famed 300,000 sacred Buddha images. It was an ordination ceremony and soon she hoped she would be among the many taking their vows at the mother temple. First, though, she had to talk with the head monk to prove she understood the precepts. After meditation this morning she would meet him for the final dialogue. She had studied the videos and read the books. She was ready.

She had transferred most of her funds to the Foundation. It was quite easy. She had signed some Thai-language documents brought by a lawyer from Bangkok. She had no money of her own, nobody did. She was free to check her accounts at the temple office any time she wished. But the money itself didn't mean anything.

Concentration eluded her that morning. It was a particularly holy day, Asaha Puja, the full moon of the eighth lunar month. There was a buzz of excitement. The most holy monks were to arrive soon for preaching. She sat with the others in meditation and after two hours of complete silence the fifty-five monks appeared and sat on the glittering dais around the *chedi*. The head monk, Phra Lokha Dhamma, read the sermon, and today, because there were so many English-speaking adherents present, he spoke briefly in English as well, in a deep, reverberating voice that seemed to carry effortlessly to the hundreds seated in rows around him. The local people present didn't seem to mind. Maybe they already knew the content by heart.

Asaha Puja commemorates the Buddha's first teaching to the five ascetics at the deer park near Benares, in India, on the turning of the Wheel of Dhamma. The senior ascetic attained the first level of enlightenment and entered the Sotapanna state of mind purity. Louisa and the other candidates for ordination at the following major ceremonies were meant to see themselves as embodiments of the ascetics, although of course they were not required to act like the ascetics of old time India, with their semi-starvation diets, filthy long hair, and horny bare feet.

On the contrary, the great thing about the Buddhist teachings at this temple was that all people and animals were meant to enjoy happy and virtuous lives and, since money was usually necessary for a happy life, the well-being of all was secured through a vast network of international investments held by the Foundation, supporting thousands of projects around the world. All projects were compatible with Buddhist teachings and still made money. At first, she had been suspicious of the motivation of the Foundation and refused to participate but as time passed, she began to see how the system worked, and to view it with awe.

It was extraordinary. Funds were invested in alternative energy, land regeneration, organic food production, new non-invasive surgery techniques, own-cell joint replacements, microbiomic treatments for irritable bowel and other gut disorders, low-cost shelter design and many other projects aimed at protecting the wellbeing of the land and all forms of life. Louisa's funds under Lokha Dhamma management had already trebled. She donated fifty percent of her profits to the Foundation and the remainder built up in her own Swiss bank account which she could claim at any time.

Although it seemed strange that adherence to Buddhist beliefs could result in increasing wealth, with her investments secure it became easier to focus on happiness and goodness. She and the other ordination candidates studied from booklets given to them at the beginning of their residence in the monastery. After hearing many sermons and engaging in many discussions she began to feel a kind of understanding. She was under no obligation to remain in Thailand, and many Foundation communities had sprung up in various countries where adherents could help others and continue to share their well-being. There was one just now being completed in the bushland near Sydney. After ordination, she planned to move there. Today's final meeting with Phra Lokha Dhamma was like an examination of sorts, and she hoped her months of study had made her ready.

It would be their fifth meeting. The first time they met she simply sat with him in the meditation hall for an hour. Neither spoke. She felt a thousand emotions pass through her. She had been told simply to observe these feelings arising and passing away. Afterwards she felt completely drained and burst into tears. On their second meeting they sat for a time but then he spoke some kind of prayer. She looked into his face and felt profound relief. On their third meeting she had been told she could ask him one question. She meditated all night on what question she should ask him, but as they sat together in the early morning light there was only one thing that lay in her mind.

"When will I find love?" she asked him, and immediately felt like an idiot.

She saw a smile cross his face, and his eyes closed.

"You cannot find love. Love must find you".

She started to ask more but he began to chant. Again,

she was flooded with feeling and tears ran down her face. When she looked up, he had disappeared.

On their fourth meeting he told her to close her eyes and walk backward around the meditation hall for an hour. At first she was terrified that she would fall over, or bang into something, not being able to see where she was going. But he told her she needed to trust her senses, so she did. She walked slowly backwards in a circle while a small bell rang somewhere nearby. Time disappeared altogether. Someone came into the hall and called her name. Phra Lokha Dhamma was no longer in the room. He could have been gone the whole time, for all she knew, but it didn't matter.

This was to be the fifth meeting.

While Phra Lokha Dhamma and the other monks took their one meal of the day in the late morning the foreign ordination candidates waited together in an airy thatched-roof shelter overlooking the sparkling pools of water. They were free to talk if they wished, but idle chatter and stupid conversations were discouraged at all times, and she certainly felt no need to talk. Then they saw Phra Lokha Dhamma climb alone to the meditation hut poised above the rushing stream. One by one the candidates were led upwards. As each completed their dialogue they left through another doorway and climbed back down to the pathway below. When it was Louisa's turn, she felt calm and ready.

'Khun Muu, Khun Muu'. Her Thai name. It meant 'Mrs Pig'.

A bank of Buddha images gleamed against one wall of the small building. On a raised dais Phra Lokha Dhamma sat cross-legged and greeted her with a kindly smile. They were silent for a time.

'And so' he began, 'shall we speak of the revered norms of the world? Can you tell me about them?'

'They are the normal conditions which repeatedly visit all worldly beings'.

'Do you understand this in your own life? The effects?'

'Yes, I think so. Although I wonder if they affect all beings, or is it only human beings? Buddhism often speaks of beings, are humans and animals the same?'

'All beings partake of the same conditions. And because beings pass from form to form through the process of rebirth, all beings share much in common, no matter what form they take in any one material existence'.

'So a cat or a dog experiences the same conditions?'

'Each in its own way. Can you tell me of the eight conditions of the world, in their correct relation?'

She had to think for a moment. 'They are the four pairs - Gain and Loss, Repute and Disrepute, Praise and Blame, Happiness and Suffering'.

'And do you recognise these in your own existence?'

She thought she had but it was hard to explain.

'I always wanted gain and was afraid of loss. Somehow, I could never gain enough, and when I did have something, I always wanted more. Then even when I had it, I was afraid of losing it. When I lost it, I felt I myself was lost. I wanted to be someone, to be noticed, to be important, but I could never achieve what was necessary. I was never good enough, no matter how I tried. I longed for praise. I could never have enough praise. And whenever anything went wrong, I blamed myself, and worse still, I blamed others for my own failings'.

The monk smiled. 'Very good', he said. 'And do you want to attain the Dhamma?'

'I do' she replied.

Then, in an even deeper voice, he intoned 'Attainers of the Dhamma do not pine over things done and gone or dream about things not yet come. They attend to the present – thus are they radiant. Do you understand?'

'I think so. But ... there is something I want to know. I want to ask. Do you yourself not suffer?'

'Yes, of course' he replied. 'All life is suffering. I suffer, just as you do, as do all beings. But the point is not to struggle to avoid suffering. Neither should you seek it. Whatever has made you suffer will pass, and then something else will come again to make you suffer, and that in turn will pass away'.

'And old age? Ugliness? Death? Decay?'

'You have great fear of this, is it not so? You have tried to defeat age, decay?'

'Yes, it is true'. Ever since Louisa had accepted that her destiny had led her here, she had been thinking about her relationship with her own body, what she had done to it.

'I wanted to remain young. I wanted to be beautiful'.

'All Westerners, and many others now, share this delusion. So many ...ladies especially. And for what reason? To attract a mate? To find love ... Even when they are already old? For what purpose?'

'Isn't it true that men love beautiful women more than ugly ones?'

'Millions are trapped in the web of illusion and the man who will love you for your beauty will stop loving you for the same reason. No creature can defeat ageing and decay'.

'Doesn't enlightenment defeat age and decay?'

'In one way. But not in another. It is wrong to think of 'defeat' in this context'.

'Yes, I suppose so. So what is it, to be enlightened?'

'The enlightened person is one who, when he is alive, is untroubled, and when he knows he must die, he is not sorrowful'.

'But how can we not be sorrowful, especially in such a terrible world?'

'Be compassionate towards those that suffer, do not add to their suffering. Remember that your goal is to live without sorrow even though we encounter sorrowful conditions'.

'And wealth? How is it possible that we should become even more wealthy while others are so poor and miserable?'

'Wealth is merely another illusion of this world. It helps people do better towards others if they have the comfort of wealth. But if they use their wealth for bad purposes it will not benefit them. Gain goes with loss. The enlightened person does not crave for gain and is happy even if he loses. So we help to create wealth while doing good for others. Those who use their wealth for evil purposes – for damaging other forms of life especially – may lose their wealth at any time, in which case, the cycle of loss, disrepute, blame and suffering may be instituted once again. It is each one's choice. Our choices pass on, from life to life'.

'How can we have choice, if what happens is already determined by our past lives?'

'You are right. No choice is absolutely free. Our existence is conditioned by past existences carried inside our cells, our bodies, even our memories. The choices our ancestors made create us as we are. Perhaps our ancestors were evil, so, we carry elements of that evil in us and we cannot flourish. But if we carry goodness from past choices, then we can enjoy better circumstances because we in turn can make good choices and help ourselves and others in our future existences'.

Louisa sat quietly for some minutes. She could hear the monk's breath, passing lightly in and out of his lungs. Everything seemed heightened, as if she had moved into some other dimension. Finally, there was her question, the one she had to ask.

'So, should it not matter, whether I find love? A partner, a lover, someone to give me love?'

'Ah, that old question again. Dear lady, do not be misled. Love is what mothers give their children to ensure their survival. All other love is the plaintive cry of the infant struggling to find once again that oceanic bliss of mother's kindness and care, of mother's adoration. You may love each other as fellow beings, along with other creatures, but the kind of love you speak of is merely illusory attachment, which can come and go again as conditions arise and pass away'.

'So I should not seek attachment?'

'When all attachments are cut off, all anxiety is driven from the heart, the heart is at rest, then peace and happiness are attained'.

'This is very hard, Master. Very hard for women'.

'Yes, women have much harder lives, it is well understood, which is why Buddhists pray not to be reincarnated in a woman's body. The suffering of women is greater because women are more sensitive. Their sensitivity is necessary so they can give the love they must give to their children, but it makes their own experiences of pain and loss so much worse. This is one of the Laws of Dhamma'.

'But surely it is not fair! It is not right that women should suffer more.'

'Only the incessant passage of the eons determines the conditions beings must encounter. We live to experience our present lives and try to do as well in them as we can. Some are very fortunate, gain wealth and security and can seek enlightenment. Others can only hope for a miserable kind of survival. The conditions have been deteriorating on this earth for over two thousand five hundred years. We are reaching the middle of the cycle, and then it will turn, and conditions will once again improve. So it is said by the sages in the ancient scriptures'.

'Do I need to study the ancient scriptures? I don't think I am very good with study'.

'Dear lady, our world is littered with ancient scriptures. Some are given the capacity to engage with them, others are not. You are struggling to find your own way to live a better life, to mitigate your suffering. You can understand the teachings of the Dhamma in a thousand ways, not only through ancient scriptures. Do you know the five precepts? Can you follow them?'

Louisa had learnt this from one of the books she had been given. It was like learning the rules for her driver's license.

> I undertake to abstain from destroying
> living beings.

> I undertake to abstain from taking things
> not given.
> I undertake to abstain from sexual
> misconduct.
> I undertake to abstain from false speech.
> I undertake to abstain from intoxicating
> liquor causing heedlessness.

She thought she could follow them.

A bell rang in the courtyard. She felt the warmth of the sun penetrating through the thatched walls.

The monk stood, smoothed his robes, and put on his sunglasses. Then, from a small bowl suspended from his waist he took a whisk and flicked her with water, saying words above her three times:

'*Namo Tassa Bhagavato Arahato Samma-Sambuddhassa*'.

He moved quickly out of the room. Her bones ached from sitting on the floor, but she felt strangely exhilarated. As she stood up, she caught sight of herself in a mirror hanging on the wall above the ranks of Buddha images. Her hair was grey, pulled back from her forehead and tied at the neck. The marks from her surgery had almost disappeared but there was something strange and stretched about her face. It resembled her, but not quite. Was this beauty? How would she have looked now if she hadn't done it?

Soon she would put on the white robes and go into retreat at the main temple. After that, who knew? She did not want to become a nun, but the idea of being a teacher or supporter and carer of others was very attractive. It felt like the right thing to do.

And after the ordination – if she qualified, and she had

no idea whether her dialogue with the Master had been satisfactory – she would get a new name. It might be Vayama, or Niradha, or Seri, or Hasapanna. She hoped it would be Niradha, or maybe just Radha. When she went back to Australia she might try again to change her name. But it didn't really matter. She understood now. Khun Muu they called her at the monastery, Mrs Pig. And after all, there was nothing wrong with pigs.

ABOUT THE AUTHOR

Born in Sydney, Australia, Annette Hamilton was trained as a cultural anthropologist. She worked in remote First Nations communities in north and central Australia. Later research in South East Asia focussed on on media, cinema and art. She now writes fiction and memoirs. Read more about her life and writing at https://annette-hamilton.com

facebook.com/Annette%20Hamilton%20Writer
twitter.com/annetteham7
instagram.com/annette_hamilton_writer